FATHER'S MECHANICAL UNIVERSE

For Kevin,
 Performing artist and
fellow literati, Live
long and well, at Walden.
 Enjoy life,
 Steve Heller
Anderson, IN
2/4/02

Father's Mechanical Universe combines the sharp, concentrated focus of a novel with the tender, lyrical quality of the best memoirs to cerate one of the most moving accounts of family love I've read in years, testifying to the remarkably high standard of Heller's work.

—*W. D. Wetherell*

Lucky Kellerman's best piece of luck is in having Steve Heller as his interpreter. The silences of the taciturn father, the oedipal urges of the visionary son, and the patience of the woman who bears with them through everything become eloquent under Heller's tender comedic gaze.

—*Marjorie Sandor*

Though I read Steve Heller's *Father's Mechanical Universe* in a single afternoon, I'm certain its magical scenes will linger in my thoughts for years to come. And the ending is perfect.

—*David Huddle*

FATHER'S MECHANICAL

Universe

a novel by

STEVE HELLER

BkMk Press
University of Missouri-Kansas City

BkMk Press
University of Missouri-Kansas City
5101 Rockhill Road
Kansas City, Missouri 64110
(816) 235-2558 (voice)
(816) 235-2611 (fax)
bkmk@umkc.edu
http://www.umkc.edu/bkmk/

MAC
MISSOURI ARTS COUNCIL

Financial assistance for this project has been provided by the
Missouri Arts Council, a state agency.

Book design by Roxanne M. Witt
Cover design by Steve Duffendack
Printed by Cushing-Malloy, Ann Arbor, Michigan

BkMk Press thanks Karen T. Johnson, Jessica Hylan, Michael
Nelson, Jeannie Irons, and Heather Haas.

Library of Congress Cataloging-in-Publication Data

Heller, Steve, 1949-
    Father's mechanical universe: a short novel / Steve Heller.
        p. cm.
  ISBN 1-886157-32-4
      1. Fathers and sons—Fiction. 2. Teenage boys—Fiction.
        3. Oklahoma—Fiction. I. Title.
  PS 3558.E47624 F3 2001
  813'.54—dc21
                         2001035002

10   9   8   7   6   5   4   3   2   1

For men who love the world with their hands, and for the women who love such men.

Also by Steve Heller

The Man Who Drank a Thousand Beers
The Automotive History of Lucky Kellerman

Father's Mechanical Universe was originally published as an issue of *The Chariton Review*.

Sections of the narrative were originally published as short stories in the following journals:

"Dreams of Heaven" in *Laurel Review*.

"Maintaining the Universe" (as "Father's Mechanical Universe") in *American Literary Review*.

"Guardians of the Sanctuary" (as "Invading the Temple") in *Great Stream Review*, recipient of the Fern Chertkow Memorial Award for Fiction.

Contents

A Note from the Author

Among the potential pleasures—and perils—of publishing a novel are the responses an author receives, if he is fortunate enough to receive anything at all, from his readers. Since the initial publication of *The Automotive History of Lucky Kellerman* in 1987, I've heard from a surprising number of readers—surprising at least to one who early on learned to value silence. For those who have remained interested in Lucky all this time, I offer this novella, intended not to extend the story of Lucky and Curly Kellerman, but to recast their tale by revisioning a portion of it through the eyes of the recipient of Lucky's legacy. For me, slipping inside Curly's skin was at times not unlike Lucky's efforts to comprehend the mysteries of his own life while constructing a classic automobile from piles of junk. Like Lucky himself, I eventually discovered the boy had grown far beyond the original dreams of his progenitor.

In June of 1995 my father, Stephen Francis Heller Sr., the man who was the inspiration for Lucky Kellerman, passed away. He is survived by my mother, Elizabeth Hale Heller, on whom the character of Babe is based. This story is a further tribute to their remarkable life together. In the wake of many significant changes in my own life, I want to especially thank one person—my wife, Sheyene Foster Heller, my first and best reader—who, together with my children, teaches me each day the reasons why one writes.

Most beautiful when they're turned off,
with scales of dirt on them, with our lives
all over them—
                                    —Robert Winner
                                    "Machines"

While pondering the infinity of the stars, we ignore
the infinity of our Father.

                              —Milan Kundera
                    The Book of Laughter and Forgetting

I

· · · · ·

A SHORT SEASON

Frank Kellerman was a man who had no words. It wasn't that my father couldn't talk; he could say things all right. Things like *Take your time, Hurry up, Hand me that wrench, No, the little one.* Father had plenty of words to name objects or describe motion, to give and refine orders. The words he lacked were the words that referred to things one couldn't see nor hear nor touch, at least not directly. Things whose existence had to be inferred or simply felt. Things like love.

When I was a very young boy I barraged him with questions about the world: *What holds up the sky? Why do girls smell funny? How come Donald Duck's voice is harder to understand than Mickey Mouse?* To these and all other difficult questions, Father had the same answer: *Ask your mother.*

Father was a sullen, inward man, with Mother as well as with me. In the eighteen years I lived with the two of them, I never once heard Father say anything to Mother that expressed any sort of affection for her. Nor did he ever demonstrate any visible sign of this. Not until I was a teenager, and had felt some of the feelings the opposite sex stirs in the human body, did I find this absence in my father strange. It was strange mostly because despite the fact that the only emotions he demonstrated toward Mother ranged from resentment to rage, I never doubted that he loved her intensely. Something in the distance he always kept from her expressed that. Something in the blank, carefully measured way he always looked at her, the way his gray eyes bulged like the eyes of a toad behind the top half of his bifocals as he stared at Mother across the breakfast table or the back porch. Those toad eyes of Father's always seemed to be looking not merely at the woman before him but also at the woman she used to be—as if by fixing his eyes on her, he was able to stare through layers of time and view the whole of their past. By my mid-teens I sometimes wondered: Maybe Father's connection to Mother was beyond love, something deeper than love. Something not even pleasant, perhaps, but stronger.

For her part, Mother never made him look ridiculous by putting on a display. She never hugged him around the neck or whispered embarrassing things in his ear. At least not in my presence. But every now and then I would catch a glimpse of something—a slight squeeze of his elbow, a lingering touch on the wrist—that betrayed the difference in their natures. Father never acknowledged these gestures.

Hugs, kisses, loving words spoken aloud, these things were reserved for me. Mother gave them freely and in abundance. And I returned them to her. And sometimes, despite his own gruff reserve, I gave them to my father. That was the pattern. Sometime in my childhood—I couldn't say exactly when—I began to feel what I could not yet comprehend: My parents expressed their affection for each other only through me.

When eventually I grasped this phenomenon, I understood something else as well: Because in the Kellerman family love flowed through me—and only through me—I held power over my parents. I could control them.

I began to control my relationship with Father in the fall of 1961, when I was almost eleven, after Father made a mistake that almost destroyed us as a family. Because of Father's mistake, and my own childish reluctance to forgive, I learned to control Father out of hate. And that might have been the end of us forever, were it not for Father's ability to communicate without words.

To appreciate my father, one had to appreciate automobiles. Automobiles were his passion—his first and only true love, Mother would sometimes claim in anger. Unlike his feelings for Mother and me, evidence of Father's passion for automobiles was easy to find; his past was documented by the various autos he'd owned during his lifetime. No, he wasn't a collector of classic cars. He was a master mechanic: owner of his own garage and autobody shop and the curator of the museum of his own personal history. Father's garage was located just off Route 66 in the small farm community of Yukon, Oklahoma, where I grew up. His "museum" was a wide, free-standing carport on our five-acre plot of land a few miles north of town. Under the tin roof of the carport he parked five automobiles: A purple 1929 Moon Prince of Windsor roadster, resting on blocks; a green 1951 Hudson Hornet ragtop; a faded blue 1954 GMC pickup we called "the Jimmie Truck"; a gleaming 1956 Studebaker Silver Hawk coupe; and, finally, at the very end of the row, a homely gray 1961 Corvair sedan.

Through these five automobiles one can trace the history of my father's adult life, the story he never told me in words. But I'm getting ahead of myself. The connections I'm thinking about now deeply involve my father, but the story is my own.

The carport Father built lay between the two-story woodframe house I was raised in and an old one-room limestone schoolhouse that was, at the time of my father's death in 1981, nearly a century old. The sign (even in my youth faded almost out of recognition) on the wood panel above the door of the entrance read "Spring Creek School." Father used the old schoolhouse as his private workshop. He spent evenings and weekends inside its walls, repairing lawnmowers, air conditioners, water pumps, anything mechanical.

When I was ten, Father broke his hip. It was in the spring of 1961, just after the start of the baseball season. The injury kept Father in bed for the entire summer—and away from the garage and autobody shop that supported us. Father became totally dependent on Mother, and hated it. She fed him, sponge-bathed him, emptied his bedpan.

For me, having Father home all day was a novelty. Over the course of that summer we grew close for the first and only time in our lives. In the morning we read the sports pages of the *The Daily Oklahoman* together (this was the summer of the great home run race between Roger Maris and my childhood hero Mickey Mantle); in the afternoon Father looked through the bedroom window and watched me stand at home plate of our imaginary ball park at the edge of Orville Zucha's wheat field and pretend I was Maris or the Mighty Mick—or Mathews or Colavito or Killebrew or Jim Gentile—and rehit the home runs the major leaguers had pounded out the day before. Home plate stood at the southeast corner of our property, and the foul lines paralleled the south and east barbed wire fences that separated our land from Orville Zucha's wheat fields. The infield was marked off in regulation Little League size, with old tomato crates serving as bases. We had no pitcher (Mother never participated in this game), so I hit the home runs fungo-style, swatting old golf balls (I was too skinny to hit baseballs very far) with my prized Mickey Mantle Little League signature bat. Depending on what had happened in the big leagues the day before, I'd smack golf balls over the left and right field fences I'd erected with stakes and kite string—or over the roof of the schoolhouse in dead center two hundred feet away. *Atta boy, Slugger*, Father would say when I'd finished my imaginary newsreel re-enactment of the previous day's home run highlights. *You're a natural.*

Father's carport formed an imposing impediment, to both the game and my imagination, in left field. If there'd been any possibility of striking one of Father's prized autos with a golf ball, the home run game would never have progressed beyond the first at bat. But the tin roof and redwood walls on the south and east sides of the port shielded Father's cars from the line drives of my right-handed sluggers. The moment I took Mickey's right-handed stance against a southpaw, the carport magically disappeared.

The home run game was the best I'd ever dreamed up. It had definite rules; nothing was arbitrary. The sports pages determined who, what, when, and how. The only thing the game allowed me to invent was the way it felt to be Mickey Mantle when he blasted homers number twenty-one and twenty-two, left-handed, off Bob Shaw in Kansas City in early June. But that was enough. Stepping into the

Mighty Mick's shoes as he dug in his cleats to face the A's tough righthander, well, that was the best thing there was.

Father understood this instinctively, though of course we never talked about it. *Nice going, Slugger* was the most he could bring himself to say about my performance. But he knew. I could see it in the way he watched me from the window by his bed, which looked onto the playing field from the imaginary stands on the foul side of the left field line. Father watched me not like a captive spectator, but like an informed fan who recognized the distinctive looping plane of Mantle's vicious left-handed uppercut, and clapped or raised his palm in salute only when I got it just right.

Then at the end of the summer—when the Mighty Mick, slowed by nagging injuries, fell behind Maris in their race for Ruth's record—Father made the mistake that changed our relationship forever. If I'd been a couple of years older and been paying more attention to how things were going outside the sports pages, I might not have been so completely stunned by Father's impulsive act. I might have expected something. For just when Father's hip had healed to the point where he could get around with the aid of a crutch, the Yukon National Bank foreclosed on his garage and autobody shop, taking away our livelihood.

On September 1st, with the start of school only two weeks away (I'd be in sixth grade), the home run race stood Maris 51, Mantle 48. Just as the afternoon tempertaure hit 102, somebody at the bank informed Father his garage had been picked up for a song by Carl Vukovich the junk dealer, Father's only real competitor in the auto repair business. I had no idea how this news would affect him.

On the day everything changed, I was playing the home run game as usual. Batting right-handed with two men on against the Tigers, the Mighty Mick had just powered one over the 461 foot sign in dead center in Yankee Stadium, right over the head of the statue of Miller Huggins, when Father's voice rang out from foul territory:

"Curly!"

As I turned toward the voice, The House That Ruth Built disappeared, and the schoolhouse, Father's carport, and the white woodframe two-story we lived in shimmered into view like heat mirages. Framed by the window, Father's poptoad eyes glimmered like twin stars behind the rectangular frames of his bifocals.

"Come here . . . I need you."

I rested the bat on my shoulder and strode over to the open window, and looked in at Father. He was sitting in the same position as usual, propped up by pillows, his right leg pulled taut by the traction weight at the end of the bed. But the look on his face was different. Determined. I knew from his voice that the game was over for the day. Nevertheless, I said: "Did you see that one? That was Mickey in—"

"Listen, son, come in here. I want you to do something for me."

When I started to go around to the back door, his voice stopped me.

"No, don't go around. Crawl right through the window here so you don't disturb your mother."

This surprised me; I was never allowed to crawl through windows. The thought didn't deter me as I tossed my bat inside and scrambled over the sill.

"Good. OK, the first thing I want you to do is unhook that weight for me."

I'd seen Mother do this when she helped Father get out of bed and limp down the hall for his bath. I grabbed the iron hook.

"Careful! Slowly . . . just ease it off . . . That's it."

I could see the muscles in Father's leg recoil toward his hip cast as I laid the weights on the lamp table. Father grimaced. He was in his mid-forties, but on that day he looked much older to me as he eased his legs over the side of the bed and set one foot, then the other, on the floor.

"Now hand me those overalls."

I helped him slip the overalls up his legs and over the plaster cast. "Where you going?" I asked.

Father winced as he moved his shoulders beneath the straps of the overalls. "To hell and back."

I stepped back and stared at him. He didn't seem to

notice. When he had hooked both shoulder straps, he said, "Now give me your bat."

I handed it to him. He planted the fat end on the floor, then pushed himself to his feet, using my bat as a short cane. This was the first time since the accident I'd seen him stand up without Mother's help. Then he took a step away from the bed. The muscles in his neck and jaw tensed. Then he forced a smile and looked at me. "OK. I'm going to borrow your bat for a while, OK?"

I nodded. "Where you going?"

"See a man at the bank," he replied as he crutched his way toward the door. "You stay right here while I talk to your mother."

That meant they were going to fight. Again. "OK," I said, and watched him limp/stagger down the hall toward the kitchen. As soon as he turned the corner I heard Mother's voice. What was he doing out of bed? she wanted to know. And where was he going? Then two words I didn't understand: *No remortgage.*

I crept down the hallway in time to see Father push open the screen door. "If there's one thing I've heard often enough to remember," he said with a snarl, "it's 'no remortgage.' So what am I supposed to do: Lay in bed while Vukovich steals my business?"

"This is our *home,* Frank. When are you coming back?"

Father released one of his heavy sighs that meant he'd had enough. "Coming back? If I don't get this note fixed, what's the point in coming back?"

Then he saw me.

"Don't worry," he said. Then, with a final glare at Mother, he turned and clumped out of the house.

I joined Mother by the sink. We watched Father make his awkward three-legged way toward the carport in the blazing sun. He picked out his most recent acquisition: the Studebaker Silver Hawk. I watched him use my bat to wedge himself into the front seat. A moment later he backed out into the gravel drive—then, without a backward glance, drove off toward Yukon.

"Is he all right?" I asked.

Mother sighed. "I don't know."

We sat down at the kitchen table and waited. Mother gave me a glass of milk. She drank iced coffee. On the black and silver formica beside her cup lay a pack of Winstons, but I knew she wouldn't touch them. I was old enough to have observed that most people smoked when they were under stress, to help themselves relax. But Mother was different. She smoked only when she was already relaxed. She liked to sit out on the back porch after the sun had gone down, when the heat of the day began to melt away before the breeze rippling through the wheat fields, and smoke one cigarette, savoring it, the tip glowing red at the end of her fingers as she propped her elbow on her knee. When she exhaled she would lift her chin an inch or so and blow the smoke in a thin stream that dissipated into the air about two feet in front of her face. As she did this, something remarkable would happen. Her heavy brow, her entire face would lighten, begin to glow like the tip of her cigarette, as if whatever worries she had carried around inside her during the day, whatever had been weighing her down, had been incinerated, then expelled in the smoke. When she was relaxed like that, often she would talk to me, tell me stories—especially if Father was inside, watching *Rawhide* or *Have Gun, Will Travel* or one of his other cowboy shows.

But this time the pack of Winstons lay untouched. Mother stared out through the screen door in silence. When I'd finished my milk, I rinsed out my glass, then went to my room and played with my army men. When I returned to the kitchen an hour or so later, Mother was sitting in the same position at the table, staring through the same screen.

At five thirty Mother called the Yukon National Bank. When no one answered, she called the bank president at home. He gave her another number, a vice president. "Yes, yes," she said to the vice president. "But when?"

After she hung up she said to me: "I think your father's going to be late."

"Where is he?"

Mother was wearing her blue cotton house dress. She turned her eyes away from me and began to brush vigorously at the lapels below her collar, as if a cobweb or something even filthier had drifted through the air and stuck to her neck. "I don't know," she said.

At nine o'clock I went to bed. Mother sat on the edge of the bed and sang me a song, "Twinkle, Twinkle, Little Star." I was several years too old for this song, and we both knew it. But she sang it to me just as she had when I was six. When she'd finished, I asked the question on both our minds. "When will Father be back?"

She managed a smile. "He'll be here when you get up."

But he wasn't. When I entered the kitchen the next morning Mother was sitting with her elbows propped on the table, her chin in her palms. Almost the same position as the evening before. I wondered if she'd been to bed at all.

"Ready for some breakfast?" she asked.

I nodded and sat down as she poured us each a bowl of Rice Crispies. She made a point of smiling at me several times while we ate, but her plump body slumped over the bowl before her. She hadn't bothered to comb her hair. She always combed her hair. This morning her hair was pushed over to one side of her head in a big brown knot. The knot just stayed there, like it was pinned on. But her eyes were what shocked me. They seemed to focus on two different points at once: on me, with a strange kind of sadness I later came to recognize as pity—and at the same time way beyond me, on some awful distant place she seemed to hope I'd never have to go.

"I think your father may have gone out of town on business."

I nodded. But I knew better. I couldn't look at her eyes and not know.

After breakfast I biked over to Cletus Bluefire's house, about a mile away down a dirt road. Cletus and I played army all morning. I stayed over for lunch, then went skinny-dipping with Cletus down at the creek. *When I get home*, I kept thinking, *he'll be there*.

But he wasn't. When I pumped my bike up the gravel drive to the garage late that afternoon, Mother was sitting on the steps of the back porch. The faraway look had vanished from her eyes; she was concentrating on me. "What do you want for dinner?" she said.

After dinner, while the sun still hung above the horizon, I read the sports page of *The Daily Oklahoman*, then went out back to play the home run game. I tried to envision the Mighty Mick batting lefty against Yankee Killer Frank Lary at the Stadium, tried to imagine Mickey fouling off hard slider after hard slider—then with his trademark uppercut smacking one off the facade high above the right field stands. But I couldn't visualize it. I couldn't get inside Mickey's body; The House That Ruth Built wouldn't materialize. My season had ended.

The next morning Mother said, "I think Father may have left us."

And so we began to adjust. Over the next few days Mother and I talked a lot about why Father had left. *The garage was his life's dream*, she explained. *Losing it was just too much for him to bear.*

But what about US? I wanted to know. *How come he LEFT us?*

For that, Mother had no answer. *It's not about you*, she kept saying. *Your father still loves you.*

I believed her. But after a while, knowing that simply made it worse. It was a greater crime, it seemed to me, to abandon someone you still loved. Where had he gone? What place was better than this? On Monday, one week after he'd left, I took a hammer and smashed the headlights in Father's four remaining automobiles. I imagined the cars were huge metal animals, mechanical dinosaurs, their headlights eyes. I blinded them, one by one. They suffered their pain in silence. The white Moon Prince of Windsor, Father's very first car, hurt the most as my hammer drove a stake through each lidless eye into its tiny stupid brain.

When Mother saw what I'd done, she demanded the hammer. I placed it in her palm. "I understand why you did it," she said. "But we've got to have something to drive."

On Wednesday morning, one week and two days after Father had left, I crossed Orville Zucha's pasture and hiked along the banks of Spring Creek until I came to an enormous willow tree that grew next to a stagnant pool. The willow was ancient, so old and decayed its gnarled trunk had split open all the way from its exposed roots to its lower branches, which drooped low over the sour-smelling pool, some of the elongated leaves dipping into the scummy water. The pool was about two feet deep in its middle, even though the creek had temporarily dried up. I wondered if there was a tiny spring somewhere beneath it. The drooping limbs of the willow surrounded the entire pool like a living green dome-shaped fortress, a safe haven.

The green dome of the willow's branches was my secret spot, the place where I came to dream my most secret dreams. Sometimes I would take off my shoes and socks and dangle my feet over the side of the thick root into the still water of the pool, and just let my mind wander. It was right here that I'd dreamed up the imaginary home run game Father and I had played most of the summer. It was this very spot where I'd imagined I'd someday bring Lila Ruzicka, the cutest girl in my class, and give her a long disturbing kiss. Inside the warm green dome of the ancient willow, anything was possible.

In the shade of the willow, I sat down on an exposed root, closed my eyes, and whispered to the drooping branches: "Come back."

When I returned to the house there was no sign of the Silver Hawk. Mother was heating a can of Campbell's tomato soup. We ate in silence.

On Thursday, because we had no other course, Mother and I turned our eyes toward the future, toward the start of school in less than a week. And toward a surprise: Mother was going back to work. "Old man Turch needs a receptionist at the funeral home," Mother said the evening after I'd smashed the headlights. "I told him I could start as soon as you're back in school."

School. I could imagine what some of the other boys, the bullies like Eddie Hacker, would say: *Hey, Curly: Heard your old man run off. He find himself another woman—or just get bored?* In the week that remained, I began to prepare myself for the taunts and the inevitable fights that would follow. I forgot Mickey Mantle and imagined myself inside my own body, a stronger body than my real body. I imagined myself freezing at the sound of Eddie

Hacker's taunting voice, then suddenly spinning to face him, eye to eye—and in the same motion driving my fist through his jawbone.

School started on Tuesday. By Monday morning, two weeks after father had left, I believed I was ready. I was prepared to fight, prepared to take a beating if I had to. If I had to spend the first day in the principal's office, it didn't matter. I sprang out of bed, looking forward to the last day of vacation. Maybe I'd bust a few taillights, just to keep up my spirits. I practically hopped my way into the kitchen—then froze.

"Daddy's home, Slugger!"

He was grinning, holding out his arms for a hug. Like he'd never left, like nothing had changed. Like it was time for us to step out into the backyard and toss a ball around . . .

Mother was standing next to him by the sink. When I looked at her she turned and hid her face.

I ran back to my bedroom and slammed the door. There was no lock, so I pushed my dresser in front of it, then crawled under the bed. Half a minute later I heard a knock.

"It's me, son."

Outside my window, the wind rose; the loose screen began to rattle.

"Everything's all right. I want to talk to you."

The wind died down again, and I heard the knob turn. From my spot under the bed I could see the legs of the dresser blocking the door.

"Open the door, Curly."

A moment later the dresser began to skid slowly across the floor. A pair of brown loafers appeared. They turned left, then right, then pointed directly at me and approached the bed. They stopped about five feet from the edge. Then, from high above, Father's voice spoke. "I want . . . I want to explain something to you, son."

From the kitchen came the sound of running water, then silence.

"I went away—I *ran* away—for a while, and that was wrong."

The voice and the shoes became still then. What did he expect me to say?

"Can you hear me, son? I still love you. Will you forgive me?"

I stared at the loafers. They were speckled with dust. I wondered where the dust had come from, how many miles from here?

"I understand," the voice said finally. "Well, you think about it and talk to me when you're ready."

The loafers twisted around then and stepped back behind the dresser. I heard the door close with a click.

Well, you think about it. What was it I was supposed to think about? Why had he come back? I wondered what he would think when he saw the blind, cowering faces of his pet automobiles. I wondered if he would bellow with rage— or cry. I hadn't cried once since he left. I was proud of myself for that. I wondered if Mother had cried, secretly in her bed at night after I had drifted off to sleep. I wondered about these and other things as I lay motionless on my belly in the shadow beneath the bed.

After a while I might have fallen asleep; I can't be sure. When the loafers reappeared, my face and arms and chest had the foggy burning ache of sleep interrupted.

"Want to talk now?" Father's voice said.

I slid back toward the wall.

"Say, I've lost track. How's Mickey doing now?"

How the hell do I know? I wanted to scream at him. *You stopped the game. YOU stopped it.*

Suddenly a fist appeared next to the shoes. The knuckles almost touched the bare hardwood floor. Then, very slowly, like the motion of a wrecking ball, the fist drew back, then swung forward. At the bottom of its arc, its fingers opened and a white ball appeared. It rolled noisily across the floor from the light into the shadow, toward me, toward my swelling eyes. I moved my arm and blocked the ball, then squeezed it in my own fist.

The shoes stood still. Then suddenly another ball appeared, rolling slowly toward me. I caught it. Then another ball, then another. Then nothing.

The shoes waited. I lined up the four golf balls along the edge of my right arm. I matched the dimples, lined up the words on each ball: Titlest, Titlest, MaxFli, Titlest. For a long time, I just stared at the balls. Then I took the first Titlest, squeezed it between the floor and my flattened palm, and rolled it back out.

"Atta boy, Slugger."

A few minutes later, I crawled out from under the bed.

II

·····

DREAMS OF HEAVEN

After his return, my relationship with Father entered a strange new stage. What must have seemed strangest to Mother was our reversal of roles. Suddenly Father was doing all the talking—*All I did was travel, son . . . I just drove and drove . . . It was wrong*—and asking all the questions—*How can I make it up to you? You want to play the home run game today? How about if I bought you a new bat, a Louisville Slugger? Is there anything you want to say to me? Anything you want to ask?* Now I was the sullen, silent one. At first this was simply the way I felt. But I soon learned the power of silence, and I began to control Father in a new way. I kept him always at a distance, made him feel the full depth of his guilt.

I'm sure I would have soon gotten over this, and made up with Father completely, except that Father made one more mistake. He lied to me. In the two weeks he'd been gone, he'd done more than drive and drive. Late that first night after his return, when he and Mother believed I was safely sleeping, I climbed the steep stairway to the second floor and squatted silently just outside the closed door to my parents' bedroom. Through the wood I overheard Father's confession. He had abandoned us for a woman he used to sleep with when he'd worked as a diesel locomotive mechanic for the Frisco Railroad. He could barely walk with the cast, and yet he had done that. *Forgive me*, I heard him say.

For a long time after that I heard nothing. It was eerie.

Then Mother's voice came through the wood. *You think it's going to be that easy? Well, it's not.* A few moments later she hurled curses at him, then something harder, something that smashed into tinkling pieces. I never discovered what it was. Then I heard the SWACK of Mother's hand against Father's face. After that I made my way back down the stairs, as silently as I'd come.

For the next few days after that Mother refused to do the things she'd always done for Father: fix his meals, wash and iron his clothes, write the checks to pay the bills. He tiptoed mutely around her, looking guilty and lost as he hunted for the Cheerios or a different shirt. Then just as I was beginning to think the change might be permanent, Mother's attitude softened. *That garage was your father's idea of heaven,* Mother remarked to me a week or so after his return. She must have understood that statement in a way that I couldn't, for soon after that she began to forgive him.

I didn't.

My reaction to the episode was strange. It should have been easier for me to forgive Father. After all, I *wanted* him home, *wanted* Mother and him to get along again. But somehow it was harder for me to forgive. Maybe it was because he'd told Mother the truth, but not me. Or maybe there was another reason. But it seemed to me Father should pay for his sin somehow—and the harsh words and awkward punches Mother had hurled at him weren't enough. When her anger faded and once again she began to cook for him, clean for him, do all the things she'd always done for him, I faulted her for it.

"How can you treat him just like you did before?" I asked her one evening while Father was taking a bath. We were doing the supper dishes, Mother and I. She washed, I dried.

"I told you," she said. She was scrubbing dried lasagna off Father's plate. "When your father lost his garage, he lost his life's dream. Do you know what that means? Maybe you'll have to be older before you can imagine what losing something that precious feels like, what it does to you inside. It changes a person. It changed your father, but he still came back to us. We should give him credit for that."

She handed me the plate and I toweled it dry. "He doesn't seem any different to me."

"Well, he is," Mother replied. "*Inside.* I just hope what happened to your father never happens to you."

In the weeks following his return we resumed our relationship, Father and I. The routine of it, anyway. And there were plenty of opportunities for us to make up. When I showed him the busted headlights on his other four beloved automobiles the day after his return, his back stiffened and the muscles in his neck clenched like a fist. His chest expanded with the fearsome rage I knew he felt. But I didn't care. I was proud of my destruction. Then, just as quickly, Father deflated before my eyes like a bellows. He gave a long sigh, turned, and said he forgave me. Said he understood how I felt.

Eventually, it must have been weeks later, I told him I was sorry I'd done it. After his hip had healed, sometimes we'd even toss a ball around in the evenings, Father urging me on, teaching me, trying to make up. *Nice throw, Slugger. Now see if you can handle this.* The smile on his face as he encouraged me was sincere but pained. He worked hard at reconciling; I have to give him that. Father was in his mid-forties then, and bald as a cue ball. I'd just begun to notice he was smaller than other boys' fathers. I was suddenly embarrassed by his bulb-shaped nose and the wire-rimmed bifocals which magnified his beady hazel eyes and gave him that pop-eyed look of a giant toad standing on hind legs. The spectacle of such a man tossing a baseball was suddenly comical to me, though I never laughed at the sight. Enough distance had emerged between us for me to see him as others might. I also saw how desperately he wanted to make up with me.

The truth was I no longer trusted him. He'd robbed me of my faith in the future, and in him. I always knew he could do the same thing again tomorrow. So I refused to make up completely, refused to make things easy for him. Sometimes I felt myself wanting to forgive him. But I wanted to punish him even more. I kept my distance. And so, by growing as sullen and wordless as my father, I exerted control.

In a way, Father never recovered from losing the garage.

He could have gone to work for almost anyone as a mechanic. We could have moved into the City; it was only twenty miles east of Yukon. But we didn't. Instead, Father took a job on the maintenance crew at the state capitol building. After that, the only automobiles he worked on were the five parked under the tin roof of the carport. To Mother's astonishment, Father kept that maintenance job, a job that was clearly beneath his abilities. His whole attitude toward work had changed. *My job is to bring home the money,* he would say whenever Mother and he got into an argument about virtually anything. *As long as there's food on the table and a roof over our heads, I'm doing my job.*

As for me, what I wanted more than anything in the weeks following Father's return was a new game, something fresh to occupy my imagination. The baseball season and the great race for Babe Ruth's home run record were nearing their respective conclusions—but after Father's return I didn't care about any of that anymore. When Father read me the sports pages—*MARIS CLUBS 57TH; MANTLE STALLED AT 53*—I hardly listened. That stage of my life was over. What I desperately wanted was someone other than Father to play with. I needed a friend, a confidant. By the time Father returned, school had started up again. So I had plenty of playmates during the day. But after school was another matter. We lived five miles north of town, and the only other child my age who lived anywhere nearby was Cletus Bluefire. Cletus's father Charley was also a maintenance man at the capitol. It was Charley who got my father the job that was beneath him but somehow too comfortable to quit. In the fall of 1961 Charley's boy Cletus was in the sixth grade, same as me—but Cletus was already twelve and big for his age, and somehow had received special permission to practice with the junior high football team, though he couldn't play in any games. So Cletus didn't ride the bus anymore, and when his father finally brought him home from school Cletus was too tired to horse around with me, even when I took the trouble to ride my bike a mile down the nearest dirt road to his house.

So to avoid a whole evening with Father after school, I'd play Explorer. Playing Explorer meant roaming on foot through the network of creeks and gullies and narrow wooded areas surrounding my parents' acreage. In all of my explorations that fateful autumn I never encountered another child. There was only one other person I might possibly run into: a strange old woman Father had always warned me never to go near.

Her name was Mabel Zucha, but everyone around Yukon called her the Crow Woman. I'd seen her at least a couple of dozen times before. An old gray-haired woman in a gray dress. She was a widow and lived with her unmarried son Orville on the nearest farm just down the road. Sometimes I'd see her walking out in the neighboring wheat fields or down by the creeks, always by herself. From a distance she always seemed to be looking for something, something she'd lost in the fields or the gullies a long time ago. One place she always seemed to head for was the old schoolhouse. Once or twice a month Father or Mother or I would catch her peeking in the windows.

"How come they call her the Crow Woman?" I remember asking Father one day after I watched him shoo her away from the schoolhouse. This was a couple of weeks after he'd returned to Mother and me. I'd asked this question many times before, and his answer had always been the same: *Ask your mother.* So I expected little in the way of a reply. This time, however, he surprised me.

"Because she thinks she's a bird."

"A bird?"

"Yeah." Father's voice was soft and low, but somewhere inside it I felt a hard edge. "Sometimes she caws like a crow. Sometimes she flaps her arms like wings."

This was news to me. I'd only seen Mrs. Zucha walking around in the fields or peeking into the schoolhouse. I'd never seen her sound or act like a bird. "How come she thinks she's a bird?"

Father removed his bifocals, wiped them off with a handkerchief, then balanced them back atop his fat nose. "Something's wrong with Mrs. Zucha's head."

"What?"

Father shrugged. "Don't worry about it. Just make sure you stay away from her."

I wanted to know more, but Father turned his back then and walked away, meaning the subject was closed. When

Father closed a subject, it stayed closed for a good while.

The next morning at recess I asked Eddie Hacker, the sixth grade bully and recognized expert on life, why the Crow Woman thought she was a bird. Eddie and I had a business-like relationship. I helped him with his reading and math; he didn't terrorize me at recess. The truth was Eddie tolerated me mostly because I was friends with soon-to-be-star-athlete Cletus Bluefire, who was already half a foot taller than either of us, and played mostly with the seventh and eighth graders. In fact, Cletus was over on the paved portion of the playground shooting baskets under the watchful eye of Mr. Underwood, the gym teacher. Eddie Hacker was actually shorter than I, but weighed about twice as much and had a flat top that was the envy of the other boys in sixth grade. My question startled him.

"You mean you don't KNOW?" he gasped.

"Know what?"

Eddie must have thought I was faking, because he grabbed my forearm and started to give me an Indian burn.

"I give! I give!" I cried. Then added: "I really don't know. Really!"

Eddie squinted at me suspiciously for several moments before deciding I was telling the truth. We were standing beside the monkey bars on the gravel and dirt playground. Eddie pulled me over by the chain link fence.

"OK," he said. "I'll tell you. The Crow Woman thinks she's a bird because she's *crazy*. Just like her husband was."

"Her husband?"

Eddie nodded. "Her husband thought he was a pigeon. He jumped off a cliff and tried to fly." Eddie paused and stared at me, waiting for a reaction.

"So what happened to him?" I asked as casually as I could manage, after as long a wait as I could stand.

Eddie rolled his eyes. "What HAPPENED? He got KILLED! That's what happened. SPLAT! Like when King Kong fell off the Empire State Building."

I was impressed. "When?"

This made Eddie smile. "The day they got married." Then the smile spread into a grin. "You know they got married in that old schoolhouse on your property."

It took me several moments to take this in. "No, I don't believe it," I said finally, risking my life. "Why'd they get married in the schoolhouse? Why'd he think he was a pigeon?"

The confusion on my face must have saved me, for Eddie did not pound me the way he always pounded every other sixth grader who disagreed with him—except of course Cletus Bluefire. Instead, he replied, "How should I know? Ask your dad."

I shook my head. "Dad won't talk about the Crow Woman."

"Then ask your mother, dummy."

At that moment an untethered tether ball smacked Eddie in the stomach. He grabbed the ball and took off after four shrieking girls who were scattering across the playground, and left me alone with my questions.

I'd previously asked Mother about the Crow Woman, of course—but she too was reluctant to talk about Mrs. Zucha. *She's a quiet lady who likes to take long walks*, Mother had once told me—but said nothing about her thinking she was a bird. So in the Kellerman house the subject of the Crow Woman had always been closed. If anyone was going to open it up again, it would have to be Mother.

I waited until after dinner, when the dishes were done and Mother and I had sat down on the steps of the back porch and gazed east past the propane tank and the wheat fields to the darkening sky above the distant ribbon of lights that formed the skyline of Oklahoma City. A special Thursday night episode of *Rawhide* was on, so there was no chance Father would interrupt us. Mother was wearing a blue cotton house dress that was rapidly fading into gray in the disappearing light. She was smoking a cigarette, holding it by the filter tip between the index and longest finger of her right hand, her elbow propped on her knee as usual. She wasn't happy, exactly. Just somehow relieved . . . purged . . . perhaps restored. As if she'd just received communion. On this particular occasion I must have taken time to study her as she sat one level above me on the porch steps, for I've carried the image with me ever since: Mother smoking, at peace with the world. Her calm made me hesitate before asking my question.

"Mom."

"Mmmm?"

"Eddie Hacker says Mrs. Zucha comes around our schoolhouse because she got married inside it."

The calm left Mother's face as she turned toward me.

"He says she thinks she's a bird because her husband thought he was a pigeon. He says her husband jumped off a cliff because he thought he could fly."

I waited for Mother to tell me to go ask Father about it. Or tell me Eddie was the crazy one. But what she finally said was, "Yes. That's all true."

In the pause that followed, I must have sensed the change that began to take place, without sight or sound, inside my head and all around me, the world I had known up to that point silently reshaping itself in the growing dark. *Yes. That's all true.* I knew there were strange people in the world, people who did very strange things. I didn't think they had anything to do with *us*.

The sound of gunfire echoed from the Motorola in the living room. A cool breeze had come up suddenly, sweeping away the last heat of the day, raising goose bumps on my arms. Mother crushed out her cigarette on the side of one of the concrete blocks holding up the steps. "It's time somebody told you all about Mrs. Zucha."

And so she did. As she spoke, her eyes had that faraway look I'd seen at the breakfast table the morning after Father left. But in my memory there's a difference. As she told me about the Crow Woman Mother's eyes looked dreamy and adventurous, as if she were looking across miles and years to a special place only privileged people could visit. Father never told me stories; he simply had no words for that sort of thing. But when she was in the mood, Mother would talk about people as if she were reading their lives out of a book. She was in the mood that evening.

"Mrs. Zucha didn't always think she was a bird," Mother began. "She used to be just like you or me. Her maiden name was Kolar and she grew up in that same farm house down the road that she lives in today. People say when Mabel was a young woman she was very shy. She was also very pretty, but in a strange, quiet way. She had lovely dark eyes and long black hair that hung all the way down to her waist. Her hair always shined like she'd just finished brushing it. But nobody ever saw her use a brush or a comb, and she showed no other signs of vanity. She was so quiet, people considered her mysterious. Especially the boys. She had a wild-eyed look like a crow, they say. But I'm not sure if that was true. People may say that now just because of what happened to Mabel later on. The only boy she ever let talk to her was a young man named Hubert Zucha. Hubert was a strange boy, as shy and quiet as Mabel. Very thin, with big round eyes as dark as Mabel's. People knew only two things about Hubert: He was quiet and he raised pigeons. They say he had a hundred of them in the barn loft on his parents' farm. Hubert trained his pigeons to fly all over the county, then come back to the barn. No matter where they flew off to, Hubert's pigeons would always come back."

"Homing pigeons!"

"That's right. Hubert knew pigeons better than anybody. I don't know if it's true, but some of the old Czech farmers say Hubert not only trained his pigeons to come back, he actually taught each baby bird how to fly."

I must have looked skeptical.

Mother smiled. "Well, that's what they say, anyway. Hubert would open up the loft doors and stand there on the edge and flap his arms like wings. And while he did that he'd talk to the pigeons. Not in English, of course. He'd say, 'Cooo, cooo.' Like that. And he'd flap his arms until finally the baby pigeon imitated him and flapped its wings. Hubert would teach each young bird just like that until finally when he thought the bird was ready, he'd toss it out into the air—and off it would fly."

"What about the mama bird?"

Mother shook her head. "I don't know, Curly. I guess the mama bird just watched. Anyway, in 1918 Hubert was drafted into the army to go fight the Germans in Europe. That was the First World War, the one your Grandpa Kellerman fought in. But after just a few weeks, Hubert was back in his loft with his pigeons. The army had discharged him."

"How come?"

"No one ever really found out why, but the story people

around here tell was that Hubert was just too strange to be a soldier. No one would trust him with a gun."

"If I had a gun I wouldn't shoot anyone except Germans and Russians."

Mother smiled. "Your Father and I hope you never have to shoot anyone, young man. Well anyway, right after the war ended, Hubert drove up in a buggy one evening, knocked on Mr. and Mrs. Kolar's door, and asked them for permission to court Mabel. That's the way they did things in those days: When a young man was interested in a young lady, he asked her parents for permission to see her."

I nodded. I knew all about this from *Gunsmoke*.

"I imagine Mabel's parents weren't too thrilled about Hubert—and maybe they would have discouraged him, except that Mabel had already put off every other young man in the town of Yukon. Hubert was the only boy left. So the Kolars let Hubert and Mabel sit in a swing on their front porch. After about an hour went by, Mr. Kolar came out on the porch to check on them. And you know what? Hubert and Mabel were gone. Disappeared."

"Where'd they go?"

"Well, that's what Mr. Kolar wanted to know. In fact, he was frightened because Mabel had never gone anywhere without his permission. So he went looking for them. He looked everywhere: down in the gullies and out in the wheat fields. He called their names, but got no answer. Finally, Mr. Kolar got in his buggy and went and got the sheriff, and the two of them searched the county. At the end of the day, about the time the sun was going down, they found them. Can you guess where?"

I chewed my lower lip and thought about it. "In the schoolhouse?"

"Good guess. But no. The sheriff and Mr. Kolar and Hubert's parents found the two of them up in the loft of the Zuchas' barn. Hubert was showing Mabel his pigeons."

"I shoulda guessed that."

"Well," Mother went on. "Well, after that the Kolars decided Hubert couldn't be trusted, so they forbid him from seeing Mabel. But then they changed their minds when Mabel informed them that if Hubert couldn't come see *her*, she'd go see *him*. Hubert was her dream man, she said."

Mother pulled another Winston out of the pack lying beside her on the step and ignited it with her Zippo lighter. She drew the smoke deep into her lungs, then expelled it in a long dissipating stream that hung in the still air like a cobweb.

"Not that Hubert was the perfect man, the man she'd always dreamed about," Mother continued. "Just that he had his own personal dream: raising those pigeons and teaching them how to fly. For Hubert, having Mabel and his pigeons up in that loft, well, that must have been just like heaven."

I closed my eyes for a moment and pictured Mabel and Hubert standing side by side on the floor of the barn loft, the loft doors open wide like curtains on a stage. In his palm Hubert holds a white pigeon. Slowly, he extends palm and bird toward the open air. Mabel and Hubert's eyes glisten as the pigeon flaps its wings, rises . . .

"Well, after that it seemed like nothing could keep the two of them apart," Mother continued. "So just a few days after that first evening, Hubert asked Mabel if she'd be his wife."

"So they got married?"

"They certainly did, though it wasn't easy. Mabel's parents still didn't like Hubert, but in the end they gave in. Another complication was the old Church of St. Francis had burned down a few weeks earlier. Hubert and Mabel didn't want to wait or move the wedding to another town, so they got married right over there in our schoolhouse. Except it wasn't ours at the time. It belonged to the township."

I watched Mother exhale. This time the stiffening breeze swept the smoke right off her lips.

"This happened back before I was born, you see, but everyone who remembers it says the wedding was quite an affair. The only words the bride and groom spoke through the whole ceremony were 'I do.' But both of them looked as happy as they could be. Mabel especially. Her eyes were full of light, everyone said. Right after the ceremony they left for their honeymoon. Hubert had rented a cabin down on the Wildhorse River near Sulphur. As they were leaving, everyone noticed Hubert had a big cage full of his pigeons packed in the back of the buggy, right alongside the luggage. Somebody yelled out 'Hubert: What are you going to do with them pigeons?' And Hubert said, 'We're all going to fly up to the moon!' Well, everyone laughed of course. And then Hubert and Mabel drove on out of sight."

Mother paused and looked at me curiously then. Perhaps I looked distracted and strange, for in my mind's eye I was beginning to dream the story as she told it, picturing Mabel and Hubert riding off in their buggy into the sunset, just like they would on television.

"Well, no one heard from the bride and groom for three or four days after that. And then the sheriff came round to the Zucha and Kolar farms with the news that Hubert was dead. The story he'd been told on the phone was Hubert and Mabel had driven their buggy up to the top of a cliff overlooking the river to have a picnic. Then Hubert opened the cage on the back of the buggy and released his pigeons. They flew way up in the sky, then down again and began to circle round and round in the air above Hubert's head. Some miners were fishing down on the river and saw the whole thing. They said the pigeons kept circling and circling like they didn't know where they were supposed to go. Finally, Hubert began to flap his arms like wings—and before they knew it, he jumped right off the cliff. He fell to his death, flapping his arms like a bird all the way down. The miners said poor Mabel watched the whole thing from her seat in the buggy."

Mother paused and looked at me, but I said nothing.

"You have to understand, Curly: That's just about the worst thing a woman could ever see. It would be like me watching your father die, or you. When they brought Mabel back to Yukon, she'd already changed. The light was gone out of her eyes. They were black, like they are now. And the worst thing was: She was already pregnant. She was going to have Hubert's baby."

I watched Mother take a slow deep drag on her cigarette. Her eyes narrowed as she stared off toward the distant lights of the City. As I watched, I continued to dream the story of Mabel's return, the light in her eyes going out. For a moment the scene in my mind's eye got mixed up: I saw Mother instead of Mabel, sitting in the buggy, smoking a cigarette. Her face looked both peaceful and sad.

"What happened to the pigeons?" I asked.

"They disappeared. For a long time people expected them to return to the loft of Hubert's barn, but they never did. Hubert's parents eventually set the rest of the pigeons free. They all flew away, and none of them ever returned, even though they were all trained to come back. It was like they all knew the barn wasn't home anymore. After Hubert's parents passed on, Ted Turch bought the old Zucha farm from Mabel. He burned that old barn down and built a brand new one right on the same spot."

I passed Ted Turch's barn every time I biked over to Cletus Bluefire's house. I'd never seen any pigeons anywhere near it.

"Nine months after Hubert died Mabel gave birth to Orville," Mother continued. "One thing I know for sure: Even though Mabel must have been very sad in those days, she wasn't crazy. You know how I know that? Because she raised Orville all by herself, until he grew up to be a fine man. And the best farmer in Canadian County. Why, during the Second World War Orville grew so much wheat for our troops that the government gave him a medal. Orville couldn't have grown up to be that kind of a man if his mother was crazy."

"But . . ." I didn't really want to interrupt her; I couldn't help myself. "What about her thinking she was a bird?"

Mother paused just long enough to give me what has come to represent in my own mind the look that defines *patience*. "Well, one afternoon about the time the war was finally coming to an end, Orville came in from the fields and noticed his mother was gone. Sometimes Mabel took long walks, but after a couple of hours had passed, Orville decided he'd better go look for her. So he searched and searched. Where do you think he found her?"

This time I knew. "In the schoolhouse."

She nodded. "Right outside it. The school had been closed for years; in fact, Orville had bought it from the township. He found Mabel staring into the windows, just like you've seen her do. She had this . . . this look in her eyes. Like she'd seen a ghost. When Orville called her name, she turned toward him and started flapping her arms, real slowly, like wings. She flapped harder and harder, like she was trying to fly. Orville was so shocked he just stood there and watched her for maybe a whole minute. Finally he said, 'Mama, what's the matter?' Then this sound came out of her throat . . ."

"Like a pigeon."

As Mother looked at me her eyes narrowed and her lips stretched wide and thin into an expression that was completely flat: neither a frown nor a smile. "No," she said. "It was a deeper, rougher sound from the back of her throat: *Haaaw, haaaw.* Like a crow."

* * *

Mother always claimed that since that day at the end of the Second World War, no one, not even Orville himself, had heard Mabel Zucha utter a single word of English. The only sound she ever made was the harsh, guttural moan of a crow. Everyone, including my father, thought she was crazy. *Something's wrong with Mrs. Zucha's head.* But ever since the day Mother had told me her story, I'd known this was not true. It was Mrs. Zucha's heart, not her head, that was hurting. I even knew why Mrs. Zucha acted like a bird. It was because of what she wanted. She wanted to find her husband. She wanted to join him.

My parents and I were all baptized Catholics, but we'd drifted away from the church. None of us had attended Mass in years, since I was nine. Nevertheless, everybody in Yukon, Oklahoma knew what happened to the soul of a good man after he died. His soul flew up to heaven. The reason Mrs. Zucha was different from everyone else was because just before her husband died she had seen where his soul was going. She had seen it—or dreamed it—in the pigeons.

I never told Mother what I learned from her story, but I think she knew I'd learned it. I'm sure other people in Yukon knew the same thing about Mrs. Zucha. They must have known. But I never talked to anyone about it. I never told anyone I knew why Mabel Zucha wanted to fly.

A couple of weeks after Mother told me the story of Mabel and Hubert, when the desire to punish Father was still ripening inside me, I saw Mrs. Zucha again.

It was early one Saturday morning. As I stepped out onto the back porch, a figure caught my eye. And there she was: standing on her tip toes, peeking over a window sill into the schoolhouse. She wore an old gray dress that went all the way to the ground, but because she was on her tip toes I could see she was wearing some kind of black leather shoes with gray stockings. Father and Mother were still in bed; it was just the two of us.

Maybe I should have just left her alone, as Father had always ordered. But in those days immediately following his return, I had learned to disobey Father. I didn't yet understand the power that I held over him, and Mother too, but I was exercising it. Still, I don't think that's what made me climb down the porch steps and creep across the yard, as silently as I could manage, toward Mrs. Zucha's back. It was because *I knew*.

When I had crept up to within a few feet of her she saw my reflection in the glass—and spun around to face me. Her eyes shocked me. They were full of black fear; they blazed with it. Beneath the gray dress her bony shoulders trembled. I'd never seen Mrs. Zucha close up before—I had never encountered an adult who was afraid of *me*. And I had no idea what to do.

Then I remembered my vision of her and Hubert standing in the loft, releasing the pigeons into the sky. Slowly, I raised my arms out from my sides, spread them wider and wider until they reached their full extension from each shoulder. Mrs. Zucha's blazing black eyes followed me, darting side to side, tracing the span of my arms. Then, just as slowly, I brought my arms back down to my sides.

For a moment nothing happened.

Then, without any warning, Mrs. Zucha stopped trembling. The fear in her black eyes vanished and she looked at me—at my face—with a different emotion, a feeling for which

I had no name. I raised my arms again, brought them down. Raised them, brought them down.

And she answered. Her bony arms spread wide, her palms opened, her long thin fingers fanned out like wing tip feathers testing the breeze.

Suddenly the bang of the screen door off our kitchen struck my ears like a thunderclap and made me jump. I turned to see Father limp out onto the back porch, yawning and scratching the crotch of his khaki pants. He rubbed his still-mending hip, then rolled his shoulders and extended his right fist in a long, slow-motion punch aimed at the distant skyline of Oklahoma City. Then he saw me.

"Curly? What you doing?"

"Nothing!" I answered, a little too loudly. "Just playing."

Father squinted at me curiously for a long moment, then nodded and stepped back into the house.

I didn't have to turn back around to know that Mrs. Zucha had vanished.

* * *

For reasons I couldn't explain, I kept hoping she would return. I stuck close to the house the rest of the day, even though it meant suffering Father's continuing attempts to make up with me: reading the sports pages, playing catch, helping him wax the Hudson Hornet, and watching as he tightened a lawn mower blade into the vice on his workbench inside the schoolhouse, then showed me how to use a flat metal file to safely sharpen the blade. The fact that I stuck around at all encouraged Father. He became animated: His voice rose with enthusiasm, and he waved his hands in broad gestures. The nostrils of his bulb-shaped nose flared. At one point he was nailing a pegboard onto the wall above his workbench, and hammered his thumb. "SONuvabitch!" he yelped, and shook his hand like a rattle in the free air. Then he looked over at me standing beside him. "It's all right, son. I'm not hurt," he said, and gave me a pained smile.

Through the whole day I pretended I was a robot, and

did what Father asked without thinking or feeling a thing. Out of the corners of my eyes I kept watching for Mrs. Zucha, but she did not return. By nightfall what had happened by the window of the schoolhouse seemed more like a dream than a memory.

The following morning, Sunday, I climbed out of bed early once again, hoping to find Mrs. Zucha peering into the schoolhouse as I had the previous sunrise. But when I stepped out onto the back porch Mrs. Zucha was nowhere in sight. I sat on the steps for maybe half an hour, waiting. But no one approached the schoolhouse.

That afternoon, about an hour or so before dinner time, after almost another full day of bearing Father's presence, I crossed the pasture that lay between our five acres and the Zuchas' farm house. I hid behind the blades of Orville Zucha's disk harrow parked next to the machine shed, and watched the house, hoping Mrs. Zucha would appear. But she didn't. After half an hour or so, I gave up and began to wander back home.

On the way I hiked through the gully of the dry creek bed that ran through Orville's pasture. This time instead of playing Explorer I pretended I was an escaped convict, pursued by the police. Bloodhounds had my scent and were catching up, close behind now. Their howls echoed louder and louder around the bends of the red sandstone walls of the gully. I had to hurry, had to outrun them, but my legs were heavy and tired. They didn't work right. As I staggered around the next bend the gully walls quickly flattened, and I came upon my safe haven: the willow tree.

The bay of the hounds echoed behind me once again, just around the last bend now—and suddenly I was crawling on my elbows, dragging my lifeless legs over the dry sand. If only I could reach the magical protective shade of the willow's branches, I'd be safe. The dry sand ground sharply into my elbows and forearms as I crawled forward. The howl of the hounds rounded the bend, no longer an echo, and I heard the approaching scuffle and heavy panting of the dogs—in a moment they would reach me. I couldn't look back. With the last of my fading strength I crawled through the drooping branches into the dark dome of the willow's fortress—

and the sound of the dogs abruptly ceased. A moment of frozen silence followed. When I finally turned around and peered back through the leafy walls, my evil pursuers had vanished.

Inside the dark safety zone I struggled to my feet for a moment, then collapsed on my back on one of the big exposed roots that curled out from the trunk in the shape of a narrow reclining chair—and rested.

I had no idea where my mind would take me this time as I lay back against the firm cushion of the willow's trunk. Recovering from my narrow escape from the hounds, I moaned with relief, then took a deep breath and gazed up toward the green dome roof of the willow—and found myself staring into the impenetrable black eyes of the Crow Woman.

I must have flinched, must have gasped, must have at least started to cry out. For in my startled vision this time she really did look crazy, squatting barefoot on a low branch about four or five feet almost directly above, peering down at me like a scavenger bird, her black eyes gleaming with their own strange non-light. Her gray toes curled over the near edge of the limb; the hem of her gray house dress drooped over the other. After the initial jolt I remember lying absolutely still, frozen not by shock or fright, but by sheer wonder at the bizarre sight above me. Mrs. Zucha was over sixty years old; I'd never seen a person her age in a tree before. How had she gotten up there? Climbed? Or . . .

I don't know how much time it took, but gradually my gaze was transfixed by something else: the expression I finally recognized in the dark luminescence of Mrs. Zucha's black eyes. She was regarding me with what my parents called *worry*.

As slowly as I could manage, I sat up on my elbows and spoke: "I'm all right."

The look in her eyes did not change as she cocked her head an inch to one side, following the motion of my body like a crow watching a cat. Peering down from the branch, Mrs. Zucha would have looked more like a bird of prey, a hawk, except for the worry in her gaze.

I swung my feet around and came to a sitting position. "I'm OK. Really."

The swifter movement frightened her. She inched away from me, away from the trunk supporting the nearly horizontal limb, like a nervous parakeet on a perch.

"It's all right," I said softly, soothingly. "I'm not going to come after you." To prove this, I crawled backwards on my knees away from the limb. "There," I said, when I'd put a body's length distance between us. "See . . . I won't climb."

She didn't seem to hear my words. Despite her nervousness, she appeared to be perfectly balanced on the limb. Her hands were balled into fists, and she bent her arms and held her fists up tight against the tips of her shoulders, extending her elbows a few inches out from her sides like stubby chicken wings. Or the wings of a baby bird.

I should have turned and walked away, and maybe that would have been the end of it. But I couldn't. The vision on the branch of the willow tree was too compelling. "Please come down," I pleaded.

She stared at me and said nothing.

I backed a few feet further away from the limb, then stood up. "Please," I said. "I won't touch you."

But Mrs. Zucha just squatted there on the limb. The worry had gone out of her eyes. She stared at me now with a different expression, one I couldn't read. She seemed to be waiting for something.

"Please come down."

She didn't hear me. My words weren't getting through. I spoke the wrong language. And once more I thought: I should leave. Just walk away. She'll climb down after I'm gone, when she's ready.

But I couldn't leave her up there. I just couldn't. For maybe a full minute we just stared at each other. Then it came to me how I could coax her out of the tree.

I lifted my arms straight out to my sides, then brought them back down.

Mrs. Zucha's black eyes brightened like glowing coals. On the limb she answered me, unfolding her own arms, stretching them to their full extension on each side. Then, in slow motion: Up, down. Up, down. A fledgling trying its wings.

I smiled and tried to look calm. The branch she perched on was maybe four and a half feet above the sandy base of the tree, about level with my eyes now, as I stood there watching her. She was sixty-one years old, but tiny, no bigger than I. If I could just get close enough, she could slide right down into my arms. I could even pull her off the branch, if I had to.

Whatever you do, don't scare her.

Still smiling, I raised my arms again and this time extended them forward, toward her. Her slow-motion flapping stopped. She looked at me eagerly now. In fact . . . was she smiling back?

Encouraged, I took a step toward the branch.

Suddenly she was in the air—*in flight*—soaring toward me, her arms outstretched . . . I had no time to brace myself. She struck me full on chest: My feet shot out from under me as I caught her in mid air. A moment later we both slammed into the earth, me flat on my back.

The impact must have knocked the breath out of me, for everything went dim, then black, though through it all I felt myself moving, twisting, struggling to draw air into my collapsed lungs. When I could see again, I had rolled over onto my knees. As I strained to suck air like a bellows, I looked up to see Mrs. Zucha bending over me—no worry in her shining eyes this time, only . . . excitement. She was *thrilled*.

"Wha . . . " I wheezed. Before I could get the entire word out, she turned and began to run—*yes, run*—out of the shady dome of the willow back along the dry creek bed. She moved astonishingly fast. *Good riddance*, I thought as I drew the rejuvenating air into my chest. Then I saw where she was heading. Up the rippled wall of a side split in the gully, toward the cliff.

"Hey!" I cried, and stumbled after her.

By the time I scrambled up to the top she was standing with her toes on the edge, facing the creek bottom maybe twenty feet below. Her arms were lifted skyward, and she raised her eyes toward the wisps of cloud floating by overhead. *No!* I wanted cry out—but stopped myself. The sound might have startled her right over the ledge. So I approached without a word, until she heard my footsteps and turned toward me. I stopped.

"Please step away from the ledge," I said.

Her eyes were black and gleaming, full of . . . what was the word? . . . *ecstasy.*

I glanced over the ledge. It was too high. "You can't do it," I said softly. "You don't know how to fly."

Her eyes blazed with black fire. I don't think she heard my words at all. She was going to jump.

"Wait," I said. Slowly, I began to step sideways, away from the ledge. She watched. *As long as her eyes follow me . . .* When I had moved about twenty-five or thirty feet from the edge of the cliff, I stopped. Then I raised my arms and extended them toward her.

To me, I said with my eyes.

She hesitated only a moment, then sprang toward me, taking long gleeful steps—hops, really: Her arms swept out, swept back, and about three steps from my fingertips she was airborne . . . this time I was braced, ready, though for an instant as she rose I thought she might soar right over my head . . . then she came down, as softly as a robin, into my arms.

* * *

And so began our private ritual. For the next four or five weeks I met Mrs. Zucha each afternoon at five o'clock, half an hour after the bus dropped me off from school but still another half hour before Father got home from the capitol. We met in the green dome of the willow. I had to be there, every afternoon. I knew that as long as I was there, she would be all right. But after that first day it wasn't fear that motivated me. It was something else. After that first day Mrs. Zucha and I communicated perfectly without words. We knew exactly what we were doing. We were learning to fly.

Although it was I who played the role of the mama bird, to this day I still don't know who was really the teacher and who was the student. The truth is, though we both knew *what* we were doing, neither of us knew *how* to do it. We were both nestlings, with no parent to kick us over the edge into our freedom at just the right moment. Instead it was trial and error, the lure of the sky versus the fear of falling. From our rendezvous point at the willow tree, we would climb up a crack in the wall of the gully then make our way along the top until we came to the highest cliff where we could spread our featherless wings against the bracing wind. In the beginning I kept her as far away from the edge as I could manage. *No,* my eyes told her. *You're not ready for that. Not yet.* Over time I taught her to race not toward me, into my outstretched arms, but beside me, as if we were two airplanes speeding down parallel runways toward take-off. Together we would run—not toward the brink and the open air like her dead Hubert, but along the cliff's edge—flapping the spindly poles of our arms like clumsy, fat-bodied birds laboring to pick up enough ground speed to catch the buoyant air beneath our awkward wings and take off. Sometimes Mrs. Zucha made the *haaaaw, haaaaw* noise as she ran. And sometimes I made it too. On my cue we'd extend our arms and leap toward the sky. For an instant we were free. But in the end gravity always defeated us. We thudded back to earth on the bald ledge of the cliff. Somehow, though, our failures didn't matter. We never gave up, not for an instant. We were bound to soar.

And so every afternoon that strange and wondrous autumn Mrs. Zucha and I looked up into the darkening sky and tried to reach it. I was certain Mrs. Zucha saw the spirit of her dead Hubert floating in the heavens above. And what did I see? I saw what I imagined Mrs. Zucha saw. I shared her dream of heaven.

In October, a few weeks after our first attempted flight, I had my eleventh birthday. Father, perhaps feeling the distance between us growing day by day, took another stab at making up. He took me to a pet store and simply let me look around. When my attention finally settled on a lump of brown fur in the very last cage at the back of the store, Father took out his check book. To this day I don't know why I decided I wanted this particular dog: a short-legged mutt whom the pet store owner claimed drank a pint of beer every night out of a pail. A Heinz 57 basset hound with a taste for Budweiser, Mr. Kroeger labeled him. I named him Boozer.

Over the next few weeks I had a great time with that dog. In the evenings we would wrestle around on the grass, play tug-of-war and toss-and-fetch. Father was careful not to horn in on our games. He seemed resigned to allowing me the distance I'd established between us. *At least he's playing again*, I once overheard him whisper to Mother. Sometimes Mother would laugh as Boozer and I played (I liked to see her laugh), and sometimes she would relax and smoke a cigarette, a Winston filter tip, the way she used to in what I was already thinking of as the old days, before Father had left, then come back. When Boozer and I had worn ourselves out, Father would go into the kitchen and return with a bottle of Budweiser. I got to pour the beer into the pail while Boozer howled with impatience and delight. Then we all sat back on the porch and watched as he submerged his snout in the bucket and lapped up the contents in a matter of seconds. Afterward, he would lay on his back and gurgle and burp and move his legs in a circular motion like he was swimming upside-down. Watching Boozer enjoy his evening brew, I realized my desire to punish Father was fading fast.

Through all this I never forgot Mrs. Zucha. Every weekday afternoon as soon as I got off the bus, before Father got home from the capitol, I would take Boozer "hunting." The previous summer Father had given me a Daisy air rifle, and he assumed we were hunting sparrows. That's how much he knew. Instead, I would lead Boozer down to the old willow where Mrs. Zucha would be waiting. The first time I brought Boozer along I was terrified he would frighten her away. So I held him firmly by the collar as we skidded down a sandstone decline into the gully.

As we rounded the bend beneath the high cliff, Boozer had his long nose to the dry creek bed, sniffing the sand. When the shaggy green dome of the willow loomed into view ahead, I brought us to a halt. Since that first day I'd always found Mrs. Zucha squatting not on a limb but on one of the exposed roots that extended like the arms of a giant squid, from the base of the tree trunk to the edge of the pool. Except for the anticipation that always shone in her black eyes, she might have been my grandmother, relaxing in her backyard gazebo. But now, as I peered through the hanging branches, I saw no sign of her. I listened for a cawing sound, anything, but heard only the rustle of red bud leaves in the evening breeze. After a minute or so Boozer got bored and began to jump on me.

"OK, boy. Let's go."

ARRROOOOOOOO, Boozer bayed as we neared the willow, and I knew he'd caught her scent. He might have taken after her like an honest-to-god hunting dog if I hadn't held his collar tight. He pulled me around the edge of the shallow pool beneath the green canopy. At the base of the willow trunk I yanked Boozer to a halt. Mrs. Zucha was still nowhere to be seen. But I knew where she was. Boozer stuffed his nose into the dark crack in the trunk, then pulled his head and howled: ARRROOOOOOOO.

"No! BAD dog!" I said sternly and yanked him away from the tree trunk. Boozer's tail curled between his legs as I pulled him back around the edge of the water to a flat bed of sandstone on the side of the pool opposite the trunk, still within the willow's sagging canopy. "Bad dog," I said again. Boozer lowered his head and let his long ears droop until they were touching red crumbly rock. I let go of the collar. "Now watch," I commanded.

Slowly, I lifted my arms, brought them down.

Boozer cowered, flattening himself out on the sand.

"No, no," I said in a softer voice. "It's all right. Just watch. This is what we do." I made the flapping motion again. Once, twice, three times.

Boozer lifted his head; his tail began to wag. This looked like fun.

I reached down and patted Boozer on the head. "Good boy."

Boozer's tongue lolled out of his mouth and he yawned.

Deliberately then, I looked up.

Mrs. Zucha squatted on a higher branch this time, about eight to ten feet above us in the dappled shadows of the leafy canopy. She peered down on us like an anxious crow, her black eyes gleaming with that strange internal light.

Trust me, I said with my eyes. I nodded at her, then turned back to Boozer. "Easy, boy," I said. "Haul in that tongue for a second." I closed his mouth. Then, holding his muzzle tight, I raised his head. "There she is."

At first Boozer didn't see her. Then I felt his body suddenly tense. "Rrrrrmmmmph," Boozer growled through his nose.

The branch above us shuddered as Mrs. Zucha started to climb higher.

"Hush!" I commanded, and held Boozer's jaws shut with one hand and slapped his butt sternly with the other. "This is a friend."

Boozer's ears drooped again. I looked up at Mrs. Zucha and smiled. She squatted back down on the branch. In the dark luminescence of her eyes I read recognition.

Ten minutes later, without a single word passing between us, Mrs. Zucha joined Boozer and me on the ground.

* * *

After that it was the three of us every afternoon in the gully. We met at the willow tree, then climbed up a crack in the wall of the gully and headed for the top of the cliff. Along its edge Mrs. Zucha and I would make our take-off runs, flapping and cawing and leaping at the sky while Boozer bound along beside us, woofing and howling with earth-bound joy.

This new game, the game of flight, was better than Explorer or even the home run game. I still don't know exactly what made it so. Maybe it was because of the wonder and delight in Mrs. Zucha's eyes as she leaped toward the sky, or the low joyous moan of Boozer baying at her side. Or maybe it was because up there atop the gully cliff the three of us formed a kind of family, the kind I needed at the time.

In early November the afternoon breezes turned cool, sweeping down from the north and causing Mrs. Zucha and I to adjust our take-off pattern. Then one Friday I got off the bus in a bad mood. Eddie Hacker had punched me in the arm. He was prompted to do this for two reasons: Because I'd made a hundred on a science test and because Cletus Bluefire wasn't riding the bus that day (his father had taken off from work at the capitol a couple of hours early to drive Cletus, the future Yukon Miller tailback, down to Weatherford to watch the high school varsity game). When I punched Eddie back—I don't know which of us was more shocked by this—the driver caught me and made me sit beside Bess Matthews, the Baptist minister's daughter, for the rest of the thirty minute ride. Bess, who looked like a potato with glasses, said nothing when I slid in beside her, just kept her thin colorless lips clamped tight and her green grasshopper eyes fixed on the back of the bus driver's neck the entire time. I knew she was humiliated inside, however, for my father was one of the more notorious heathens in the county—and in fact had once told Bess's father to go fuck himself when he showed up at our door, Bible in hand, to invite us all to Sunday services. I actually might have felt sorry for Bess having to sit next to me, if my mind hadn't been totally occupied with anticipating the consequences of my own foolish reflex in response to Eddie's punch. Over the next dozen miles of dusty roads, Eddie sat behind us and snickered—remembering, no doubt, how Bess once reported that her father referred to Eddie and me as "Satan and his servant." In desperation, I began to fantasize: Maybe the sight of Bess and me imprisoned in the same small cell would be revenge enough for Eddie. Maybe he wouldn't want to beat up on me at all. The thought grew like another dream of heaven in my mind.

When Eddie got off three stops ahead of me, he whispered in my ear: *On Monday you die.*

Five winding miles later, when I finally got off, Boozer was waiting by the mailbox. He leaped on my chest, attempting to greet me with his usual slobbering four-footed embrace. "Down!" I ordered, and pushed him off, then stomped toward the house. "I hate school!" I screamed at Mother after kicking open the back door. I slammed my books down on the kitchen table. "I don't want to go back to that stupid school! I HATE it!"

"You have any homework?" Mother replied.

I looked at her and saw a face as stone hard as the walls of the old schoolhouse across the yard—the same face, I realized some years later, that Father gazed upon each time he angered her. Mother was the compassionate one in the family, but if you treated her shabbily she could get tough in an instant.

"It's not due till Monday," I pleaded.

In my angry pout it took me a good hour to finish my English and math. By the time Mother decided Boozer and I could go hunting (this time I had to beg her for permission), it was almost time for Father to arrive home from the capitol.

"Dinner in thirty minutes," Mother warned. "Don't be late."

When I stepped off the porch and turned the corner of the house, I noticed the sky darkening to the west. A storm front, miles away and hidden from Mother's viewpoint in the kitchen, was moving toward us. I called Boozer, who came running from behind the propane tank. As we crossed the highway to Orville's pasture, I saw Father's ugly gray Corvair, the only car he ever drove now since his return from Afton, cresting the next hill.

"Come on, boy. Let's hump it."

I wasn't sure Mrs. Zucha would still be waiting for us. We were more than an hour late. Did she have other things to do? Or would she even notice the time? Did she check a clock every afternoon before she left Orville's house to rendezvous with Boozer and me at the willow tree? Or was her sense of time strictly instinctive? As we hurried on toward the gully, I forgot about my father and Eddie Hacker and Bess Matthews and stupid homework and everything else that had been on my mind.

When Boozer and I rounded the last bend and the willow finally came into view, I saw the figure of a woman sitting beside the tree trunk. From this distance, in the soft dappled light spearing through the canopy of drooping branches, she could have been any age. A grandmother or a young girl. This time she did not squat like a bird on a limb, but sat patiently on the exposed sofa-shaped root, absolutely still in her long dress, her hands folded neatly in her lap. Then she saw us. Instantly she perked up, rose from the root like a graceful young woman who'd just been asked to dance a waltz. Her dark eyes flashed with anticipation in the dappled light, and she smiled. It didn't matter we were late. Mrs. Zucha was ready to fly.

We climbed up the side of the smaller intersecting gully to the top of the nearest cliff. Up there on the bald cliff, to my surprise the western sky was already closing in: a wild, tumbling black and gray. The breeze had stiffened in advance of the roiling clouds, and the temperature had already dropped maybe ten degrees, making me shiver. Except for the soft shoosh of the wind through the branches of the nearby maple and red bud trees, the air was strangely quiet for all the motion in the sky. On the distant horizon, well behind the turbulent front, a tongue of lightning licked the earth. The storm was only minutes away now. Boozer raised his snout and sniffed the air, then began to whine.

I looked over at Mrs. Zucha. Her dark eyes were turned away from the approaching storm toward the lighter sky to the east, where a flock of black birds soared on the edge of the wind toward Oklahoma City. And I realized: She didn't sense the storm at all; all she felt was the cool fluid cushion of air that could lift her, lift us both, into the sky.

It was my decision. I was the lookout, the protector. All I had to do was clap my hands together to grab her attention, then gesture toward Orville's farm house to indicate today's flight attempt was over. Then start walking toward my own house. Mrs. Zucha would head straight home. She always did. For the very first time I grasped the true nature of my role in our game, the role of the mama bird: I was to decide not what but when.

I turned and faced the advancing wall of clouds. The storm was still minutes away; home was close by. We had time for one brief run toward the sky.

Boozer yapped and howled while Mrs. Zucha and I limbered up, checking out our wings: up, down, up, down. Mrs. Zucha was wearing a gray shawl over the shoulders of her faded blue, almost gray dress. She held a tip of the shawl in each fist, and when she spread her arms wide in the chilly breeze the fringe of the shawl fluttered like wing feathers. Watching Mrs. Zucha lean her frail body into the wind, I thought of those old drawings of birds that artists had made for the men who designed the first machines of flight, machines powered not by aviation fuel but by muscle and sweat—machines made by men who were building not airplanes but birdmen.

Without warning, from the bottom of the gully exploded a sound—heavy and sudden as a blast of thunder: *CURLY!*

I lurched backward, the force of my own name almost knocking me off my feet. I regained my balance in two seconds, just in time to see Mrs. Zucha twist and stumble—the shock of the word had caught her full force—toward the edge of the cliff. I wish I had seen her eyes, the look in them, for she was still flapping her arms as she stepped over, the shawl expanding and billowing behind her back—and for an instant I thought: *This time she might do it: Catch the wind and rise.*

Then she was gone.

I don't know how long it took me to bring myself to the edge. When I finally looked down over the twenty foot precipice I saw two figures. Mrs. Zucha sprawled flat on her back on the soft brown sand of the creek bed, her arms and legs spread wide, fanning out her gray shawl and her long blue gray dress, making her look like a faded snow angel. For a moment, maybe the longest moment of my life, she did not move. Then her fingers curled, uncurled. Her head rolled a few inches, toward the sky, and her eyes opened. From where I stood trembling, the spots of her eyes looked not black but opaque, as if the fall had knocked the blackness out of them. She stared up into the churning heavens with a look that saw nothing.

Bending over her was the man who had called us both back to earth.

Father looked up at me, and I saw his own eyes were full of fear. "She's OK," he said. "She's OK."

He knew I didn't believe him.

Abruptly the wind died. A hush fell over the gully as the limbs of the maple and red bud trees along the cliff relaxed. I might have turned, looking back toward the west for the black undulating cone of a twister, if the two figures below hadn't held me transfixed. Mrs. Zucha's eyes had cleared; her gaze focused on Father now, who knelt over her like a woodland priest delivering the Last Rites. Her eyes shown with—what was it?—recognition. As if she saw, truly *saw* him, for the very first time. But it was not he that she saw. Only the sudden calm allowed me to discern the single faint word that issued suddenly from Mrs. Zucha's lips as she gazed up at Father:

"Hubert."

Father's torso quivered. He said nothing, then slowly shook his head.

The light in Mrs. Zucha's eyes faded out.

* * *

She lived. The ambulance took Mrs. Zucha to Baptist Memorial where the doctors discovered she had suffered a broken collar bone and eight broken ribs. Over the next few weeks we visited her four times, but on each occasion she was sleeping and did not awaken while we were there. In sleep Mrs. Zucha looked like a corpse: her small face colorless and gaunt, its sallow wrinkled flesh sagging off curved bones of her skull. *We'll see her when she gets out,* Father promised. I wondered if she would ever come home. Or, if she did, would she be the same person, my special friend?

While Mrs. Zucha was hospitalized something else happened that I wouldn't understand until years later. Late one night a vicious electrical storm exploded outside my window, scaring me out of a deep sleep. A driving rain began to roll down the glass in waves. The hall phone rang. A moment later I heard Father's heavy steps clump down the hallways toward the ringing. Silently I crept out of bed, opened my door an inch, and peered at Father's shadowy figure through the crack. "Yes, operator," he said groggily into the hall phone. "This is Frank Kellerman." When a flash of lightning lit the hall I saw his face in profile. His face seemed expressionless, like the face of a cadaver. But he gripped the phone tightly in his fist like a hammer. When he finally began to speak, his voice was so low that with the thunder rumbling and crackling outside I couldn't pick up what he was saying. Lightning continued to flicker. Father kept shaking his head as if the person on the other line could see him plain as day. The person on the other end of the line apparently was pleading—or demanding—that Father explain something he'd said, some decision he'd made. But Father almost never explained anything. At the very end of the conversation his voice rose.

"No . . . Just plain no . . . I'm sorry."

He hung up, and I slipped quickly back into bed. A moment later he looked in on me. I kept my eyes closed, pretending to be asleep. About half a minute passed before the door clicked shut again.

The following morning Mother waited until after Father had left for work, then told me the news: My Grandpa Kellerman had died of liver failure. The funeral would be in two days—but we weren't going.

I rose from my chair at the kitchen table and let my spoon plop handle-first into the bowl of Wheaties. "Why not?"

At that point I'd never met either of my grandparents on Father's side, which had always struck me as odd, since they lived in Kansas City, which was only about a day's drive from Yukon. In his curt way, Father had always spoken fondly of Grandma Rose. But when I'd once asked Father what Grandpa Joseph was like, he'd given a one-word reply on which he refused to elaborate: *Mean.*

Mother set down her coffee, then gave me a pained look and said, "You really ought to ask your father that."

We both knew that was pointless. If anyone was going to explain something in the Kellerman house, it had to be Mother. So I stood across the table from Mother and rocked back and forth on my heels, waiting her out. I knew I wouldn't have to wait long.

Mother made a sad face that told me I was going to get an explanation, not a story. "When your father was a boy," she began, "your Grandpa Kellerman brewed bootleg beer. This was during Prohibition when it was illegal to make or drink anything alcoholic. But your grandpa drank a lot, and he abused your grandma."

I felt my eyes pinch down into a squint. "Abuse" was a

word I'd heard used only in connection with children. I wasn't sure what she meant.

"He beat her up," Mother explained, reading the confusion on my face. "Sometimes with a belt. Sometimes with his fists. And sometimes he did this in front of your father."

I sank back down into my chair. I'd seen photographs of them, Grandma and Grandpa Kellerman. Grandma Rose was a round woman with a round face. Her hair was thick and short and hugged her head like one of those old leather football helmets. In all the photographs she looked worried but determined, like a woman staring into the face of an approaching storm. Grandpa Joseph was a short, bitter-looking man with tiny eyes. In every picture he wore the same clothes: a white shirt and dark pants with dark suspenders. This fact made me wonder about the belt Mother had mentioned. Unless it was only for . . .

"What did Dad do?"

Mother shook her head. "He couldn't do anything. He was just a boy, like you."

I bit into my lower lip and tried to imagine the scene as Father must have experienced it. But in my mind's eye, something strange happened. Instead of picturing Grandpa and Grandma, I saw instead a nightmare vision: Father, slapping a skinny black leather belt—his own belt, the belt he wore every day—against his palm. His face was sober, business-like. Then I saw Mother: cowering, her own face bloodless with terror, her palms open and extended as she backed into a corner. *No,* she pleaded. *No.*

I swallowed and made the image disappear. I was only eleven. This was just too horrible, too *personal*, to absorb. And too unfair. I'd seen my parents argue a thousand times, of course. Vicious fights, some of them. Fights that scared me. But in all their fights I'd never seen Father raise a hand against Mother.

"He used to beat your father too," Mother continued. "For nothing. For disobeying him. For being a boy."

Her face had an angry but faraway look, as if she were remembering something she'd seen with her own eyes rather than reporting what Father had told her. But she couldn't have seen anything. She didn't know Father when they were children. They hadn't even met.

"And he did something else that your father has never been able to forgive."

My eyes widened. Something *worse?* "What?"

She shook her head, then gave me a look I recognized. A look that said: *This is as far as I go.* "If you want to know the answer to that, you're going to have to ask him yourself."

I believed her. But there was another question I had to ask. "But Grandpa's dead and Grandma Rose is still alive. How come he won't let us go up and see *her?*"

Mother looked at me with sympathy, but didn't answer. We had gone as far as words were going to take us. The rest was silence.

We didn't go to Grandpa Joseph's funeral, and Father never explained why. But six months later, after Grandpa was safely in the ground, Father drove us up to visit Grandma Rose in Kansas City. After that, we visited her regularly, at least once a year. In all those visits, Father never once spoke of his own father, and he never took us to see his grave.

As the years rolled by, I began to suspect that there were occasions when talking only made matters worse. Words, I decided, could be more terrifying than life. Words made you see beyond what was actually there to see; they let you imagine the horror behind the act. Even though I was desperately curious about what grandpa had done to Father when he was a boy, I was afraid to ask. Mother's words had made me feel the deep and abiding power of what words themselves couldn't touch.

At some point I might have conquered my fear, but I had another reason to keep my question to myself. By the time of Grandpa Joseph's death, I knew Father well enough to realize that if he wanted me to know what had come between the two of them so long ago, he would tell me on his own. So I didn't ask. He never explained.

In the months that followed the phone call from Kansas City, as we all speculated whether or not Mrs. Zucha would ever fully recover, I kept another related question to myself: What kind of a man would go to a hospital to visit an old woman he thought was crazy, and not go to his own father's funeral?

* * *

Six months after her fall, Mrs. Zucha's broken collar bone and eight broken ribs had healed well enough for her to come home from Baptist Memorial and live once again with Orville. Orville did not permit visitors. *Thanks for your interest*, he'd say whenever we tried to see her. *But Mama's resting.* Another six months passed. Then one day Father, to his own relief this time, discovered Mrs. Zucha tiptoeing once more around the schoolhouse. *Look, she's back!* he cried from the porch. But by the time Mother and I had scrambled to the window, she had vanished.

When the news got around that Mrs. Zucha was once again prowling her old haunts, the citizens of Yukon knew how to interpret it. *The fall hadn't affected her at all*, people said. *She's still the Crow Woman.*

But they were wrong. Mrs. Zucha was back all right; I soon caught a glimpse of her myself, peering into a window of the schoolhouse just as she always had before our practice flights above the gully. The sight of her made my chest heave. I started to call out to her in my own crow's voice: *Haaaw, haaaw.* But before the sound left my lips, she spotted me. And without as much as a nod, she vanished, disappeared around the corner. For a long time I stood there on the porch, staring at the empty space she had left.

I thought about walking down to the gully, to the willow tree, to see if she waited for me there, as she had so many times before. But I never did. I knew it wouldn't be the same.

In a way, maybe the citizens of Yukon were right. Maybe after her fall Mrs. Zucha was more the Crow Woman than ever. Maybe she was truly the Crow Woman for the first time. But she and I were no longer connected. After her fall, whenever Mrs. Zucha looked upon me—and it was never for more than a second or two when I happened to turn around in the yard and find her peeking at me from around a corner of the schoolhouse—the expression in her eyes was one of confusion and fear, as if I were someone whose face she vaguely recalled, someone who had done something terrible to her a long, long time ago.

In the year following Mrs. Zucha's fall, some things changed and some things remained the same. Just a few days after her fall, Boozer was run over by a coke truck. For some reason I blamed Father. We buried Boozer in the back yard next to the mulberry tree. After that I stayed away from the gully altogether. And for a long time I refused to speak to Father.

Although I caught regular glimpses of Mrs. Zucha over the next six years, until I'd grown up enough to finally leave home for good, the sight of her flapping her spindly arms never again made me want to soar toward the heavens. And because she no longer appeared to recognize me, the guilt I felt over what had happened at the cliff gradually faded from my day-to-day thoughts. After a time I began to believe it had completely disappeared.

III

·····

MAINTAINING THE UNIVERSE

Of the five automobiles in Father's private collection, I was told the story of only one. It was Mother of course who told me.

Two years had passed since Father's return; I'd just turned thirteen. By this time Father had stopped trying to talk to me, had given up on words altogether. We had grown equally silent, communicating with each other mostly through Mother. *Your father wants you to . . . All right, tell him I'll be there in a minute.* Our mutual reticence around each other now seemed natural; we were comfortable with it.

One unusually warm October evening I was helping Mother with the dishes. She washed; I dried. Above the tap we stared out the window at the stubby bald figure of Father carrying a bucket of soapy water toward the Studebaker Silver Hawk, which he had backed out from its stall beneath the tin roof of the carport.

I'd observed this scene many times: Father caring for his beloved automobiles (He'd long since replaced the headlights on all five of his beauties). Maintaining my distance, I'd begun to comprehend Father's view of the world. Father's vision was clear and simple: The universe was a giant machine. Not like the atomic clock in my *Pathways to Science* textbook, but like an ancient automobile that had to be fueled, maintained, restored. And driven. Anyone could drive it, I realized. Driving it was the easy part. All you had to do was decide where you wanted to go, then steer a true course. The hard part was keeping the engine running. Keeping it from breaking down, falling apart. Dying on you.

But as I watched Father sponge soap on the broad hood of the Silver Hawk, I could see his relationship with his private universe was more complicated than that. He moved the sponge like a man who was bathing a beautiful woman. Father *loved* the machine. Not just cars, it suddenly struck me, but the whole strange world. Every stick and bone of it.

But why?

As I watched Father wash the Silver Hawk, I asked Mother a question.

"Which of Father's cars is your favorite?"

On the edge of my field of vision I saw Mother's eyebrow go up. I usually made a point of ignoring Father's automobiles; this was one of the ways we maintained our distance.

"My favorite?" she repeated finally. "The Hudson."

"How come that one?" I asked. In my view, the Silver Hawk was by far the prettiest of Father's odd old cars. The gray Corvair he drove every day now was clearly the ugliest, and the old blue GMC pickup we called the Jimmie Truck was the least interesting, the one your eyes would skip past as you scanned the row of automobiles. The most exotic-looking vehicle was surely the ancient Moon Prince of Windsor: a bright purple horseless carriage fit to carry cartoon royalty. When I was younger I used to imagine Scrooge McDuck riding in the back seat of the Prince of Windsor, Scrooge's bespectacled face serenely happy as Huey, Dewey, and Luey drove him down the grand avenue toward his money vault.

"Because your father bought it about a year after we got married, the same time he bought the garage in Yukon," Mother replied, handing me the platter with the pink roses in the center. "Those were maybe our very best days . . . your father's and mine, I mean."

I made no reply, for I recognized the wistful tone in Mother's voice, the tone that signalled she was going to tell me all about it.

"That was way back in 1951, when you were just a baby. Your father hadn't worked a single day since before you were born—in fact since before we'd gotten married. Almost three whole years, since he'd had that accident when he was working for the Frisco."

I nodded as I toweled off the platter. Both Father and Mother had told the story of Father's railroad accident numerous times over the years. I had all his injuries memorized: broken arm, broken leg, seven broken ribs, severely strained back. The doctors had to stitch him back together with wires. I tried not to frown as I thought of this, for the railroad injury reminded me of the summer when Father had broken his hip and everything had gone bad.

I looked through the window. Father was sponging the taillights of the Silver Hawk with a delicate circular motion, like he was polishing crystal.

"The first few months after the accident were a nightmare," Mother continued. "Your father was so broken up inside he could hardly talk and couldn't eat at all. They had to feed him through his veins at first. The doctors in Fort Scott weren't sure he'd be able to walk again, much less go back to work. After two months they moved him down to Oklahoma City where they had physical therapists who could maybe do him more good. I quit my job at NABISCO and moved down there just so I could see him every day. Eventually they gave me a job right there in St. Anthony's, I was there so much. I'd been a nurse's aide during the war, so there was plenty I could do to help out. I tell you, Curly, it was rough, even with me by his side. Those first couple of months, I think there was only one thing kept him going. Something Pete Yuri said to your father when he came to visit at the hospital."

I raised my eyes. This was new. "What?"

"He said 'Sue the railroad.'"

If I'd been a year or two older I might have smiled at this. Mother's face, however, was dead serious. "That was how he got the idea for his garage. Your father was a great diesel locomotive mechanic, but cars were what he loved. Well, he got him a good lawyer, and three years after the accident the Frisco settled for seven thousand dollars." She paused and took a breath. "Seven thousand dollars was good money in those days. Not enough to make you rich, but enough to let you dream big. Your father was out of the hospital a whole year before the check finally came. He got disability pay, but the truth is I supported us that whole time. We got married the day after he got out, you see."

Mother's eyes grew distant again as she rinsed the last glass, then handed it to me. The glass was cool, and I realized we'd been doing the dishes in slow-motion. The hot water had run out.

"I think it was the dream more than the fact the money was coming that made your father decide we should finally get married. The dream drove us both, you see. Your father wanted his car repair business, and we both wanted a home and a family. We were going to have all three, courtesy of the Frisco. While the lawyers were still arguing about how much and when, your father and I moved into a little house in Midwest City on the edge of Tinker Air Base. That was two years after the accident, and he still had to have a crutch under each armpit just to get around. I'll swan, he'd been in physical therapy every day for . . ."

Her voice trailed off. I said nothing and kept twisting the glass around the fulcrum of my towel-wrapped fingers, twisting and twisting the glass like I was machine tooling it, shaping it to precise specifications.

"Ten months later you came along," Mother abruptly began again. Her gray eyes flickered as she looked over at me and smiled. "And then—*finally*—the check arrived. Three thousand five hundred dollars. The other half went to the lawyers. So after all that we didn't have enough money to actually *buy* anything, you see. What we wound up with was just enough cash to go into serious debt. But we were committed; your father had already picked out that garage in Yukon. The day the money came he gave the Yukon National Bank a down payment. The next thing he did was take out a mortgage on this house and five acres from Orville Zucha. And the third thing he did was talk Orville into driving us all over to Coogan's Motors in Bethany so he could buy that Hudson Hornet."

I looked at the long beetle-shaped backside of the green Hudson ragtop parked between the shocking purple Prince of Windsor and the baby blue Jimmie Truck. The sun was setting now, and the low refracted angle of the light cast the contrasting colors of Father's auto menagerie in sharp relief.

"English racing green," Mother said, as if she'd been reading my thoughts. "The Green Hornet, that's what your father called it. It was the prettiest car on the lot, by far. Sometimes I say your father's car crazy, but that's not really it at all. A man whose business was caring for automobiles, well, that man had to drive a car that said who he was. It wasn't really pride—or even ambition. The Hornet was part of the way your father saw himself, saw all of us, I think. When he drove us away in the Green Hornet, he said to the whole world: *We're not settling down; we're moving on.*"

Mother fell silent. I stopped twisting the last glass and plopped it in the dish drainer and stared through the window at Father who was now rinsing the gleaming Silver Hawk with a hose. Until Mother's revelation I'd never thought of Father as a dreamer. I'd thought of him as a sour old drudge, a man dedicated to sweat. *Life is work* had always been his unspoken message to me.

"What about the other cars?"

Mother did not reply until I had turned back toward her and once again we were eye to eye. This time I saw something else in her face, something that startled me. We were confidants, Mother and I, especially on this day. But there were limits, boundaries between us. Her eyes gazed on me from the other side of a translucent wall. The gate had snapped shut.

"If you want to know about the other cars," she said, "you're going to have to ask your father."

"All right," I replied. "I will."

A moment later I stepped out onto the back porch. From this distance the sharply contrasting colors—Concord grape, English racing green, baby blue, shining silver, and dull homely gray—made Father's automobiles look like toys. Four of them—the Prince of Windsor, the Green Hornet, the Jimmie Truck, and the gleaming Silver Hawk—were clearly prized possessions, carefully maintained in vintage condition like scale models displayed behind glass. The fifth, the battered gray Corvair he drove every day, bore the scars and bruises of a life of hard labor. But it too was clean, and ran like a frisky quarter horse.

Why those particular cars? I wondered. *Why did he buy them? Why'd he keep them all this time?*

Father had shut off the hose and was dragging a chamois across the hood of the Silver Hawk, licking up every drop of water, as I approached.

"Dad," I began, and observed his nonreaction as he deliberately kept his eyes on his business. I called him Dad whenever I wanted something, and he knew it.

"Mmmm?" he hummed finally.

"When'd you get this car?"

"Nineteen fifty-six."

I waited another ten seconds to see if the question inspired a further response, but it didn't. "You buy it new?"

"Yep."

Father was squatting beside the fender on the driver's side now, pulling the chamois down over the silver skin of the Studebaker, going with nature, as he called it. He was wearing a dirty white T-shirt, and I could see him shift his shoulders to keep the downward pressure equal in both hands. The movement caused him some difficulty; there was a hitch in his motion, the legacy of his broken hip. Or was it the broken ribs? Or the wrenched back? Or something else Mother hadn't told me about?

I watched him circle the entire automobile, removing with relentless awkward strokes every tear streaking the sides of the Silver Hawk, before I spoke again.

"How come you bought this particular car?"

This time he looked at me, clearly surprised by my continuing interest. These questions violated the distance we always kept between us. I wanted something; that much we both knew. But that was all. We studied each other. Sweat speckled his forehead and dripped off his bulbous nose. His nose had an unnatural hump in the middle. Always too big for his face, Father's nose had been broken in a fight when he was a teenager. Mother had told me about it, how Father had fought a boy twice his own weight—and taken a terrible beating. When I'd asked Father about how his nose got to be so big, all he'd said was *Never hit anybody in the face.* I wondered now what else he'd had broken over the years. I wondered if one time or another he'd broken every single bone in his body. I wondered if he thought his injuries made him more or less of a man.

"I bought the Silver Hawk because it was the best car of its time," Father said, then surprised me by continuing. "And because 1956 was the best year for me and your mother and you. Things were going good for us then; all we had in front of us was an open road." Behind the bifocals Father's poptoad eyes had that same faraway look in them I'd seen on Mother's face the day after he'd abandoned us.

"What made this car the best?"

The faraway look dissolved as he focused his gaze once again on me. We hadn't played these roles in years: me the questioner, he the answerer. I could see him struggling to find the right words in response. *Don't ask me to ask Mother,* I pleaded silently.

Suddenly Father reached into a cardboard box at his feet, then handed me a smooth dry cloth and a can of Turtle wax. "You want to know about this automobile, you help me make it beautiful."

I looked at the cloth. "All right."

His eyes flickered at my response. I never volunteered, never agreed to help except under threat. Then his face turned gray and business-like.

"Don't use too much wax," he said, and showed me how to dip the cloth into the can.

I polished the silver metal until my shoulders ached. By the time we finished, the sun had slipped beneath the horizon and the western sky had faded from gold to gray. The Silver Hawk gleamed even brighter than before, however. Or so it seemed. The chrome trim made the car look sleek as a jet fighter. I imagined the Silver Hawk streaking across the darkening sky.

"There," Father said, stepping back to have a look for himself. "Now that's the way she looked the day I drove her off the showroom floor."

"I believe it."

Father's eyes may have flickered again as he glanced at me. Or maybe it was the angle of the fading light. "Throw everything in the box," he said. "Let's go in."

I frowned at him. This wasn't fair. "But aren't you going to tell me about the car?"

Now Father's eyes narrowed, the way they would when he took his measure of me. "I'll do better than that. I'll show you."

Before I could even wonder what he meant by that he pulled a lever and raised the hood behind the forward-thrusting, puckered lips-shaped grill. He pointed at the clean gunmetal gray engine. "You know what that is?"

"The motor."

Father chuckled. "That's more than a motor, son. That's a Packard V-8 with Ultramatic transmission. A true classic. The fifty-sevens had blown Studebaker engines—forced induction—but they couldn't begin to compare to these Packard V-8s." He shook his bald head with the full certainty of his conviction.

I knew nothing about forced induction, or anything else about engines, as Father understood all too well. But instead of giving him a bored stare I gazed down at the V-8, then back at Father, waiting for him to say more. But he didn't. Instead he reached down and pressed his thumb against the fan belt. "MmmmHMMMM," he hummed. Then he grasped my wrist and, overcoming my surprised resistance, guided my own hand down to the proper spot and closed my fingers around the belt. "All right now, tug. There . . . feel that? Feel it wiggle?"

Father's grip on my wrist was firm but also gentle, flexible, sensitive to the responsive pressure and motion of my own hand, as if he were a master surgeon guiding me through a delicate operation. Inside my palm the belt moved maybe a quarter of an inch. I nodded.

"Right! That's too much play. We're going to have to tighten it. Open up my tool box there and get me that ratchet wrench. Hurry it up. OK now, hold it like this . . . That's right." His fist closed around mine as together we applied pressure to loosen the bolt.

And so it went, Father's narrative of touch. In the beginning his hands guided my hands more than my thoughts. But, gradually, with the mute caution of a reluctant apprentice, my mind began to pursue the new rhythms of my body. And as we worked together tightening the belt, my hands following his hands, I began to feel something—something for which even today, decades later, I have no name. Perhaps what I felt was not contained in the smooth steel of the wrench, nor the stubborn resistance of the bolt, nor the slightly too slack tension in the fan belt, nor the slumbering power of the Packard V-8— not in the machine at all. Perhaps what I felt was in Father himself, something for which he too had no words, but every intention of imparting to me. Whatever it was, it stung me—burned its way through my blood until it had scorched my entire body, inflamed each cell, each nerve. I wondered if he could feel the heat radiating from my hand. If so, he gave no sign.

It took maybe fifteen minutes, or perhaps it was longer before Father was satisfied the tension on the belt was just right. Somewhere along the way I felt the flame inside me subside. I calmed down. When the bolt was set in its final position, Father let me tighten it without his help.

"All right, let's try it," he said when I handed him back the wrench. "Get behind the wheel and start 'er up."

I blinked at him.

"Make sure it's in park."

I opened the door and sank into the soft red leather bucket seat behind the wheel. Father stood beside the fender. "OK," he said.

I turned the ignition key: The big Packard V-8 growled to life like a trained bear. Father lowered the hood, then came around to the driver's side window.

"Wanna drive it?" he asked.

I felt my face flush. I'd never driven one of Father's cars before. Nor any car, for that matter. I was big enough, though; my feet reached the pedals easily. I'd watched Father behind the wheel many times; I knew what to do. I was at the age when my mind travelled places my body couldn't go. I ached to go, and Father knew this. I turned and looked at him. He was looking right back at me, but stood erect beside the car, wiping off his hands with a rag. About four feet from my shoulder.

"Sure."

Without another word, he stepped around to the passenger's side and got in. I stared at the highway stretching out beyond the gravel drive toward Yukon to the south, Piedmont to the north. Dirt roads crisscrossed the highway at each mile marker.

"Where should we go?" I asked.

Father rolled down the passenger's window, propped his elbow on the sill, and gazed straight ahead through the perfectly clean, perfectly clear glass of the Silver Hawk's windshield. "Anywhere," he said.

IV

· · · · ·

GUARDIANS OF THE SANCTUARY

After teaching me how to drive, Father attempted to draw me deeper into his universe by making me his apprentice mechanic. Father had received his own education from Otis Schmidt, a master mechanic in the West Bottoms section of old Kansas City. Otis had shown Father the secrets of the internal combustion engine, the manual transmission, the differential, and the universal joint. In inviting me to help him care for his beloved automobiles, Father intended to pass these secrets on to me.

But I resisted. Despite the thrill I'd felt behind the wheel of the Silver Hawk, the way driving down dirt roads with red Oklahoma dust boiling up behind me seemed to open up the world, the laws that governed Father's universe seemed to me too rigid and unforgiving. If you let metal touch metal without proper lubrication, there would be friction. If you overinflated a tire, it would burst. If you filled your tank with gasoline that contained inadequate octane, your motor would knock. Even with proper maintenance, everything eventually rusted, decayed, stopped, or died. In the end, everything was junk. That was the overriding law of Father's universe.

During the two-year period I served as Father's apprentice I decided that we lived in two different universes. To use the language of the science fiction stories I read at the time, the universes Father and I occupied were parallel but incompatible. We occupied the same time and space, but in a certain sense we did not touch. The parallel universe I occupied was mystical. For me, life was mysterious, awe-inspiring. The most important things in the world were invisible. The reason why Mickey Mantle was a great ballplayer that I should want to trade places with—and Roger Maris was not—could not be observed on the playing field or in the locker room or the record book or anywhere else. The force that drove me to dream of kissing Lila Ruzicka beneath the branches of the old willow tree down by the creek was not physiological but spiritual. I wasn't really convinced that some-time in the next century I would have to die. Anything was possible and nothing was ever adequately explained, for the power that fueled my universe was magic.

By the time I was fourteen and a half, Cletus Bluefire already had his learner's permit and was about to vanish into a different universe altogether. But before he became a man of wheels, Cletus and I had been fellow amateur sorcerers. When a problem confronted us we dealt with it by consulting our secret oracle: a flattened horny toad that Cletus's father had run over with his pickup truck. Cletus kept the oracle in a Muriel Cigars box. *O Seer from the Other Side,* we would chant over the oracle's corpse. *Give us the courage and wisdom to ace Mrs. Pribyl's biology test.* Sometimes the magic worked; some-times it didn't.

By the time my fifteenth birthday approached and I was taking driver's ed. at Yukon High in order to get my own learner's permit, through my apprencticeship I'd begun to pick up some of the wisdom of Father's universe. I knew how to check fluid levels, replace spark plugs, change oil and filter. Basic maintenance. But two things were increasingly clear to me: I had little interest in machines, and Father had no belief at all in sorcery. We were each alien in the other's universe. Despite this fact, I'd begun to secretly wonder if some kind of miraculous bridge could be built to connect Father's universe with my own (maybe my learner's permit or perhaps my unrestricted license at sixteen could accomplish this), when suddenly my apprentice-ship was cut short. Not by Father, nor by my own disbelief, but by determined intruders. Intruders who were alien to us both.

After he'd lost his garage and autobody shop, the schoolhouse had become Father's special place to tinker on things mechanical—anything that moved or conducted an electrical charge. He worked late into the night after work and on weekends: fixing, cleaning, tuning. From my parallel universe I began to envision Father as a kind of rustic American Dr. Frankenstein, passionately reconstructing broken machines, reanimating them—restoring not mere utility, but life.

As part of my apprenticeship, Father regularly invited me inside his private sanctuary in order to teach me custom, ritual, and lore. I discovered that on this one subject, the ruling passion of his life, Father could actually speak at length. *The '51 Hudson Hornet was the king of the stock car track, son. Six cylinders, one hundred forty-five horsepower. Nobody could touch it. Here, put your finger right there and prop open that valve . . . That's right. Now hold it steady while I turn this screw.*

The schoolhouse was Father's universe in miniature: One room of organized chaos. Stacks of boxes, cardboard and metal, slouched against the plaster walls like crumbling columns of an ancient ruin. Each box bore a crudely scrawled label: METRIC TOOLS. PIPES. NUTS. WASHERS. WIRE. Etc. Scattered over the floor on grease-stained bath towels and Century 21 Realty doormats were Father's various larger projects: the driver's side door of the Silver Hawk, the interior panel removed to expose the warped guide rail that made the window difficult to roll up or down; the Cold Spot water heater with the leaky tank; State Senator Hyman Boscoe's window unit air conditioner, the one with the noisy fan. These objects lay in various stages of dissection, their respective parts spread neatly on the proper towel or doormat, awaiting Father's reanimating touch.

Against the east wall stood a sink, toilet, a turn of the century ice box, and a kitchen counter on which rested a hot plate. Meaning that Father's retreat was self-contained, capable of sustaining him and his projects in complete isolation over substantial periods of time. The hub of Father's workshop, the axis around which all objects in his universe turned, was his worktable. The heavy oak slab, longer than a picnic table, sat against the south wall, beneath a window where Father would have plenty of sunlight. For close work, Father couldn't have too much light, so from each corner of the table retractable lamps extended toward the table's center like tulips reaching for the setting sun. In the precise center of the table one would always find Father's current main project, the latest test of his mastery of the rules and regulations of his mechanical universe.

In the first week of October, 1965, when I'd begun to dream seriously about what kind of automobile I'd like to own and drive, the brightest object in Father's constellation of projects was the two-barrel carburetor of the Hudson Hornet, the one with the sticking valve. I was assisting Father in a delicate operation designed to reanimate the carburetor, holding my finger on the valve precisely as he had instructed me, when the walls of the schoolhouse began to hum . . .

I believe Father felt the vibration, the violation of his sanctuary, before either of us heard the sound. Father was bending over the valve in the intense light of the window and the four directed lamp beams. Beads of sweat sparkled like sequins on the pink and gray dome of his hairless skull. Abruptly he raised his head, then stood erect and looked around the room.

"What's the matter?" I asked.

He turned and peered down at me above his bifocals. "What's that?"

"What's what?"

Then we both heard it. Soft at first, a faint quiver, a distant buzz like the sound of electric hair clippers in another room down at the very end of the hall. Only there was no hallway and no other rooms. As we listened the sound deepened to a low hum. It seemed to come from all around us, a heavy, throbbing, monotonous vibration.

Father took a step back away from the table. "What the hell?" he cried—and his eyes widened. At the same time the light began to fade, casting his face in shadow.

I turned to look where he was looking, toward the window—and gasped. Through the rectangular frame I saw a blur of motion like the frenetic movement of bacteria beneath the lens of a microscope.

"Bees," Father said. "They're swarming into the walls."

"But how . . ." The question died on my lips, for in my mind I'd already provided the answer. The ancient limestone walls contained numerous cracks between and through the individual stones. The space between the stone and the interior plaster held no insulation, only air; there were plenty of crevices and hollow spots to accommodate bees. The plaster walls themselves were scored by dozens of cracks.

"But if they can get into the walls, they can get—"

A blur in front of my eyes snapped off the rest of my sentence. "Yaaaeeeee!" I shrieked—and swatted wildly at the bee trying to land on my nose.

"Hey!" Father yelled, and with one well-timed swipe slapped the bee out of the air. "That'll show . . ." Then he too broke off in midsentence, as another bee and then another buzzed out of a large crack next to Father's worktable. He grabbed an oily cloth lying next to the carburetor.

"No . . . goddamn . . . *intruders!*" Father cried, snapping the cloth at the bees. "Keep the hell out of here!"

But they were pouring in now: Through all the cracks in the south wall, tens, hundreds of honey bees, filling the schoolhouse with their whirring sound and motion.

"Let's get out of here!" I yelled. But Father stood his ground before the emerging cloud of bees, desperately flailing the air with the rag like a station master straddling the tracks trying to flag down a runaway locomotive rumbling straight for him. I grabbed Father around the waist and began to yank him toward the door.

"All right, all right!" Father finally conceded as the air around us turned yellow then brown with the swarming cloud. I brushed a bee off his back as we bolted through the door.

Outside, at a safe distance, we checked each other carefully: *On your hip! Your hip!* Father found three crawling on the backs of my pant legs. Finally, when we were certain we'd swept each other clean—no bees inching toward collar or cuff—we took a deep breath, then turned and gazed back at the schoolhouse.

"Sweet Jesus on popsicle sticks," Father said.

The swarm, about six feet in diameter, boiled like lava erupting from a fissure in the center of the south wall. The constant motion of the honey bees, yellow with dark bands, made the swarm appear to glow in the sunlight, changing color from yellow to brown to gold, moment by moment.

I shivered; I'd never been this frightened. When I was four I'd grabbed a honey bee off the blossom of a wild flower in the back yard. The sting had caused my right hand to puff up to one and one-half times the size of my left. This despite the fact that Mother had immediately pasted my entire hand with Arm and Hammer baking soda to neutralize the venom. *Might be the boy's slightly allergic to bee stings*, Doc Enos said in prescribing an anti-toxin. A week or so later, after the swelling had disappeared, Mother had me tested at the Yukon Clinic. It turned out I was no more allergic to bee stings than the average person. Nevertheless, my memory of the white blotches and searing pain persisted long after the visible evidence of the sting. From this experience, in my own mystical universe I'd come to believe two things: One honey bee could cause incredible pain. A swarm of honey bees could kill.

Suddenly Mother was beside us. "What's going on?"

"See for yourself," Father said, and gestured toward the schoolhouse.

Mother shaded her eyes from the sun and peered at the south wall. "Well, I'll swan! Were either of you stung?"

I shook my head.

Mother blew a deep sigh. "You were lucky. Let's get inside the house before they decide they don't like the accommodations."

That sounded like an excellent, a superb idea to me. But when Mother and I had taken five or six steps, we noticed that Father hadn't moved.

"What's wrong?" Mother asked.

"That," he replied, and pointed at the swarm. "That's what's wrong."

"What are you going to do about it?" Mother asked. Now she was frightened; I could hear it in her voice.

Father didn't even look at her. "That's my workshop," he said. "They got no right to it."

Mother stood where she was, but lowered her voice. "Of course not, Frank. But you can't do anything about it right now. You'll have to call in a beekeeper."

Father stared at the swarm. "Maybe. Maybe not."

* * *

For over an hour Father stood in the yard about forty feet from the south wall of the schoolhouse, watching the swarm. Another hundred feet across the yard, from behind the screen door to back porch, Mother and I watched him.

"I don't like this," Mother said. "He's planning something."

Almost as soon as the words were out of her mouth, Father suddenly turned and walked over to the carport and climbed into the cab of the Jimmie Truck.

"Where you going?" Mother called through the screen as he backed out onto the gravel drive. Father looked at her for a moment and winked—then hit the gas and roared off toward Yukon.

"I don't like this," Mother said. Her face had a cold gray look of foreboding resignation. She knew very well how Father was when he made his mind up about something. She'd lived with it half her life.

"What's he going to do?" I asked.

She shook her head. "I've no idea. All I know is there'll be nothing we can do to talk him out of it."

Half an hour later Father returned. He pulled up next to the back porch and unloaded two large chemical fire extinguishers. Mother said nothing, just folded her arms across her chest and stared at him.

"What are those for?" I asked through the screen.

Father looked at me, then pointed back toward the schoolhouse. "That swarm on the wall there's getting smaller by the minute. Know what that means?"

I shrugged.

"It means they're settling into the walls—or the inside of the schoolhouse. They're settin' up house in there. If I don't get rid of 'em now, I might never get rid of 'em."

I chewed my lower lip and stared at the two red cylinders.

"That second one's for you," Father said.

Mother shoved between me and the screen. "The hell it is. He's not going anywhere near those bees."

Even as petrified as I was of the bees, this action embarrassed me. After all, I was nearly fifteen. "Mom," I said gruffly, and stepped around her until my nose was practically pressed against the wires.

"See," Father said, beaming with triumph. "The boy can make up his own mind. Here." From the back of the pickup he grabbed a pile of something bright yellow and tossed it onto the porch. I peered down at the items: a heavy rubber coat, hood, and a pair of matching pants. "Hank down at the Fire Department loaned 'em to me. There's a set for you and a set for me. I got the gloves and boots too. Not to mention *these*."

I raised my eyes to see Father holding up what looked like a pair of ladies' nylon hose.

"I didn't want to borrow any of Her Highness's undergarments, so I bought these at Del Mar Drugs. What you do, see, is put on the hood . . ." Father pulled the yellow hood over his head to demonstrate, then stretched the opening of one of the nylon leggings. . . . then pull the hose right on over it like this. There. Bee proof."

"Oh, for Christsake, Frank. You look like—"

"I'm talking to the boy," Father snapped.

I felt Mother set her jaw as she glared at him.

Father removed the hood so he could look me in the eyes. "Well, what do you say?"

I stared past him to the yellow/brown/gold mass roiling on the limestone wall of the schoolhouse. "You're going to spray the wall?"

"That's right, son." Father waited for about three seconds, then added: "From the inside."

I melted back away from the screen. "You're going back inside the schoolhouse?"

Father rubbed a palm across his forehead. "We're trying to drive them *out*, not in."

I looked down at the gear, then back at Father. What kind of a man would do such a thing when he didn't have to? This made no sense, no matter what universe you happened to live in. "Mom's right," I replied finally. "You should call in a bee-keeper."

Father shook his head. "We can take care of this ourselves."

He waited, but I dropped my gaze to my shoes, shifted my weight from one foot to the other.

"Fine," Father said, and began to pull on the rubber pants.

Two minutes later, he was ready: Hood, hose, coat, pants, boots, and gloves all in place. "Check me," he said, rotating slowly. "See any exposed areas?"

"You look like a banana popsicle," Mother said.

Father stopped rotating, then picked up the first fire extinguisher. "If I'm not back in a week, send me a postcard."

I turned to Mother. "Tell him not to do it."

Mother shook her head. "He's past listening."

Now I was angry at both of them. "This is *stupid!*" I snapped. But Father had already turned and was striding toward the schoolhouse. Mother spun away from the screen door, then stepped back to the hallway and picked up the telephone.

"What are you doing?" I yelled at her.

Mother didn't look at me as she dialed. "I'm calling an ambulance."

I blinked at her, then turned back toward the schoolhouse. Father was rounding the corner of the schoolhouse toward the door on the west side. A moment later he disappeared inside. "I can't believe this," I muttered. "I just can't believe it."

Mother was giving directions to our house. Then I heard the phone click. Mother's footsteps approached from behind. "Get the baking soda out of the refrigerator," she said.

I remained where I was, staring at the swarming blob on the stone. From this distance I could just hear the faint humming beat of their wings, like the deep whine of a heavy machine in a factory.

Suddenly the hum deepened. The churning blob on the wall seemed to pick up speed, changing colors with the speed of a strobe light. A moment later a yellow blur burst from the west side of the schoolhouse, then raced across the yard toward the house.

"Get the baking soda," Mother repeated.

* * *

Father was stung six times: twice on the neck, the rest on his arms. By the time the paramedics arrived, Mother had applied baking soda to each sting. Father's neck swelled up as thick as Mickey Mantle's. *He'll be OK; we've seen worse,* the paramedics said. Nevertheless, they administered anti-venom intravenously on the way to Baptist Memorial. The doctor in the Emergency Room admitted him for twenty-four hour treatment and observation.

For most men this might have meant the end of the battle or at least the beginning of an armed truce. But Father wasn't the sort of man to take a defeat lying down. A week later, when he'd recovered both his strength and his will, he attacked the bees again—this time with smudge pots, intending to smoke them out. He succeeded in stinking up the schoolhouse and staining the ceiling black. Next he tried bug spray, then various types of poison mixed with sawdust to look like pollen. The bees seemed to thrive on it, and their numbers grew. Throughout all of this I maintained my distance, figuring it was better to disappoint Father than to risk my health over a swarm of bees. But Father persisted. Over the following months he stuffed flypaper and no-pest strips in the cracks. Then he tried caulking. Then cement. Six months and three more stings later, he finally gave in and hired a professional beekeeper to steal the queen and cause them to swarm out of the walls.

By then the hive had spread throughout the south wall, in the gaps betweens stone and plaster. The wall was slowly filling up with honeycomb, giving the schoolhouse an eerie sweet smell.

The beekeeper came early one Saturday morning. Father, in an unusually cautious mood, watched from the back porch. At noon the beekeeper emerged from the schoolhouse and approached us. He removed his hood and shook his head like a man without a clue.

Biggest natural hive I ever saw. They're spreading into every wall, you know. I knocked four holes in the plaster, and every time I managed to get close to the queen, they move her to a new spot. I think we may have to tear down the whole east wall—least ways a good many of the stones—to get 'em all out of there.

I turned and saw a change come over Father. His eyes, for the last six months burning with lust for revenge, shone with an entirely different emotion. One I couldn't quite place.

"Thanks," he finally said to the beekeeper, "but that won't be necessary. How much do I owe you?"

* * *

On Sunday Father said hardly a word all day. That evening a special re-run of *Have Gun, Will Travel* was telecast, but Father sat through the entire episode with the sound turned down so low Mother and I could hardly hear it from the back porch. "I don't like this," she whispered to me while the concluding theme played. "He's thinking again."

On Monday morning I rode the bus to school as usual. My learner's permit (I'd scored 100 on the written test) did not allow me to drive any of Father's automobiles by myself. That afternoon Cletus Bluefire, who by this time had his unrestricted license, gave me a ride home in the beat-up, body primer-colored GTO he'd resurrected from Carl Vukovich's auto graveyard.

Mother had the oven door open, poking at a roast with a long fork. I dropped my books on a chair. "Where's the old man?"

Mother kept her eyes on the roast. "He's in the school-house."

I stared at her to see if she were serious. When she said nothing, I stammered, "The bees . . . are they . . . "

"Oh, they're still in there, all right. With your father."

I looked back through the screen. The swarm had disappeared after the second day—the bees were all inside the walls and in Father's workshop now. "Did you call for an ambulance?"

She shook her head. "No need."

I frowned. "How long's he been in there?"

"All day."

"What? Jesus, he could be dead!"

Mother lifted the platter from the oven shelf and carried it over to the table. "Nope. He shows himself in a window every now and then, waves to let me know he's OK."

"What? What's he wearing—a space suit?"

"Nothing. His regular clothes."

I stared through the screen door, then back at Mother,

who was now stirring something on the top of the stove. I recognized her mood: Resigned disapproval. She wouldn't try to stop Father, but she wouldn't accept his behavior either. "What do you mean, 'his regular clothes?'" I asked. "What's he doing in there?"

She raised her eyes from the pot and looked at me. "Sharing. He's sharing the schoolhouse with the bees."

"*What?*"

"You heard me. This morning he walks in the kitchen and tells me he's been going about this all wrong. 'War only causes suffering,' he says. 'Share and share alike,' he says. Then he pulls out a pie pan, fills it with about two inches of tap water, then pours a quarter pound of sugar in it and stirs it all up. 'You tame more bees with sugar than smoke,' he says. Then he takes the pan and marches over to the schoolhouse and steps right inside. I haven't seen him since, except in the window."

"But," I could hardly get the words out, "what's he *doing* in there?"

Mother dropped the spoon in the pot. "I believe he's fixing that carburetor on the Hudson. That was his intention. He must be having a little trouble with it." When I gaped at her, she shrugged her shoulders and said: "He's their *roommate*."

I sank back against the wall. "This isn't happening."

Mother heaved a deep sigh, then stared out the window toward the schoolhouse. She looked at it for a long time, her hands braced on her hips. As she stared at the schoolhouse her mood seemed to darken, the look in her eyes growing more intense and willful, as if she were deciding to do something about Father after all.

Finally she turned toward me. "Look, I want you to do something for me. He left the door of the schoolhouse wide open. 'Might as well,' he says. 'Who's gonna come in?' Well, I want you to get as close as you can to the door without attracting any bees, then yell in there and tell him something for me."

I took a deep breath to prepare myself, then nodded. "What?"

"Tell him dinner's ready."

* * *

I did precisely as she asked. The schoolhouse door was wide open, just as she'd said. I positioned myself a good fifteen feet from the entrance. Bees were flying in and out of the doorway; I could hear quite clearly the deep pulsating burr-rurr of their wings throbbing through the walls as I yelled: "Dad! Dinner's ready!"

A few moments later, Father appeared in the doorway. He was wearing a white T-shirt, khaki pants, and what my buddies in tenth grade called a shit-eating grin. The nostrils of his already-too-big-for-his-face nose, that nose some unnamed childhood bully had broken with his fist, flared with pride.

"Well," he said, spreading his arms to encompass the extent of the world he'd reclaimed. "Whaddaya think of *this?*"

"It's great, Dad. I'm happy you're alive."

Father wrinkled his brow. "*Alive?* Son, I'm *thriving.*" He lifted his arms above his head and hop-danced a complete circle. "See? Not one sting. I've tamed the bees: We're partners now!"

I let a breath escape my lips too quickly. "Partners?"

Father dropped his hands and the pitch of his voice. "Sure. Look, they've got their job to do, and I've got mine. As long as we keep our minds on our work, we get along just fine."

"What's their job?"

"Making honey, of course."

I could smell the pungent sweet scent from where I was standing. "I see. And your job?"

Father snorted, his nostrils shuddering like a pony's. "Same as it always was, of course. This is my workshop; I've just decided to share it with a few co-workers."

"A few co-workers."

"Well, all right. Quite a few."

At that point my mouth must have been hanging open. "Dad?"

"Yeah?"

"There's a bee on your shoulder."

Father turned his head slowly to his left. The bee was crawling toward his bare neck. Father reached up his right hand and placed his index finger between his neck and the bee. With no hesitation, the bee crawled up onto his finger.

"That's right, honey."

Honey?

"Stand aside, son."

I took half a dozen quick steps to my right.

Slowly, Father lifted his finger off his shoulder. The bee fluttered its wings, but remained on the finger as Father brought his arm out to its full extension, straight ahead, pointing finger and bee toward Orville Zucha's pasture across the highway. "OK, now get on with your business." Father flicked his wrist: The bee catapulted off his finger into the air, made a quick loop, then flew straight for the pasture.

I stared incredulously at the bee until it disappeared, then turned back to Father, whose arm remained outstretched, his finger pointing decisively toward the pasture.

He gave me a wink and said, "Babe Ruth calls his shot."

I took a deep breath. "Jesus, Dad."

Father dropped his arm and laughed. "Nothing to it, son. You know, I was stupid trying to drive the bees out of here. I didn't know what they were. I didn't understand their nature. But now I do. We're a lot alike, you know."

"You and the bees."

"That's right: We both have our projects, and we need this place to work on 'em. No reason why we can't work together in peace. Wanna see?"

An arrow of terror speared my chest. "What?"

"Come on inside and see for yourself. See what we're up to. The bees won't hurt you, I guarantee it. I've tamed 'em."

The look on my face must have answered him louder than my silence.

"Seriously, son: I've already got 'em trained. I feed 'em sugar water and control their flight paths from the walls to the pan. I've been in there with them all day. I'll show you where to stand; you won't be in any danger." He took off his glasses and stared at me with naked pleading eyes. "Come on in for just a minute. Will you come?"

I thought it over. I listened to the drumming buzz, smelled the sharp musky sweet scent, watched worker bees fly in and out of the cracks in the limestone. I reminded myself that what Father had already accomplished with the bees was in my eyes incredible—perhaps even magical. In his own parallel universe Father was a scientist. He had already tested his hypothesis and concluded: *No danger.* But in my mystical universe, the bees were alien invaders. They had exotic formidable weapons and might do anything. The hair on my forearms stiffened as I felt the tingly magnetic pull of Father's private cosmos. I wanted to reverse the polarity, find the point of intersection, the window in the magnetic storm—whatever it was the spacemen did in the science fiction stories I've since forgotten—and step through the invisible barrier between us.

I turned my sorcerer's eye inward, in search of the magic that had served me so many times before. *O Seer from the Other Side, give me wisdom and courage sufficient to this task.* A few moments later I reopened my eyes and spoke.

"I'm sorry, Dad. It's your hive, not mine."

Father gazed at me a long time before replying. He was more than disappointed; it was obvious he sensed defeat. Then his expression changed. His eyes took on the determined, faraway look of a man about to embark on a long journey to a distant land only he believed existed. "That's OK, son," he said finally. "Don't worry about it."

He smiled then (or was it a wince?) and raised his hand in what might have been a salute or a wave or some other gesture of parting—then turned swiftly on his heels, stepped back through the doorway into the humming industry of his workshop, and disappeared.

V

·····

THE POWER OF SILENCE

And so my apprenticeship came to an end before I'd learned the most important secrets of Father's universe, the secrets that compelled him to love the life he labored ceaselessly, like his bees, to maintain. This was my choice. Father's workshop, though occupied by aliens now, remained open to me. *The bees are fully trained now, son,* Father assured me. *They're not invaders; they're guardians. They're my honeys.*

Time proved he was right. To my knowledge, once the bees became his honeys Father was never stung again. Not once. Mother was never stung either—but like me, she stayed clear of the schoolhouse.

With each passing month Father withdrew deeper into his private sanctuary. His universe became invisible to Mother and me and everyone else who knew him. His honeys kept it hidden and increasingly mysterious. During the day Father labored for his paycheck at the capitol; in the evening after supper he vanished behind the throbbing walls of his workshop. No monastery provided a more secure cloister.

Not even Mabel Zucha, who still regularly roamed across Orville's pastures and wheat fields and onto our five acres, approached the schoolhouse now. The bees both fascinated and terrified her. Occasionally I spotted her observing the burring activity around Father's workshop from a safe distance behind the mulberry tree or the propane tank or Father's carport. If a bee came near her, she would immediately flee. But for as long as she managed to stay wide of their flight paths, she would gaze intently—longingly, it seemed to me—at the schoolhouse, perhaps recalling the day she had married Hubert inside its walls, or maybe wondering if some sign of him could still be found there. Her eyes glistened with the same vague faraway look I'd noticed in Father's eyes the day my apprenticeship ended.

But that wasn't all. Whenever I happened to get close to Mrs. Zucha (I made no special effort to approach her; after all these years it would have felt like an invasion of her privacy), I noticed something else as well. After a few minutes of watching the schoolhouse her gaze would shift to the bees streaming in and out of the cracks in the limestone. Her eyes began to follow their flight paths. It seemed to me she admired, even envied, their determined passage through the open air. Her black eyes followed them, studied them like a young bird observing from the nest its hovering parents. If she had then spread her arms like wings, perhaps I would have recognized my old playmate—and perhaps she would have recognized me. But her arms remained always limp at her sides. Instead of trying to fly, after watching Father's honeys for a while—if she hadn't already spotted me and dashed away—she would follow the flight of a single bee until it buzzed out of sight. Then she would stir from her hiding spot and stroll off, casually but quite deliberately, in the direction the bee had disappeared.

Sometimes I wondered if Mrs. Zucha's wanderings took her down to the magical shade of the old willow tree above the stagnant pool, where the two of us used to escape into our own separate imaginary worlds. But I never followed her across Orville's pasture to check. I was afraid I'd find her on the cliff.

After my refusal to join Father in his sanctuary, the old distance between us re-emerged. At first I told myself the gap separating us had less to do with events than with the fact that we were simply two different kinds of people, aliens who could not find the secret passageway to each other's cosmos. But I soon had to admit my own universe was rapidly changing. Or, rather, I was now traveling faster than the speed of light through space and time, toward the edge of something new.

By the time I turned sixteen and got my unrestricted license I found myself following Cletus into a third universe, one that was neither mechanical nor magic. For me, auto-mobiles began to represent status, freedom, power. The means for adventure. I wanted nothing further to do with Father's old clunkers, as I began to refer to them. I wanted a car of my own, one that expressed who *I* was, something I'd picked out all by myself.

To achieve this, I got a job sorting mail at the Yukon post office after school. After a year I'd saved more than enough for a down payment. On my seventeenth birthday I decided to buy myself a present: A two year old 1965 cherry red Corvette Stingray.

The Vette was flashy and mean, with a 427 cubic inch V-8 under the hood. A real monster: a sleek sweet shark. Not the old man's style at all, and I knew it. He'd spent the last month counseling me on how to shop for an automobile. Oh, he had plenty of words on this topic. *Don't fall in love with speed and power*, he cautioned. *Don't be swayed by chrome and metallic paint. People judge a man by the car he drives. So stay within yourself, don't brag.* That was his wisdom and advice. Never a word about what I wanted.

On Saturday morning, my birthday, I listened to Father's lecture, then drove out to Alan Merrill Chevrolet on Route 66. I was in control. I'd already talked Mother into co-signing the loan and the insurance papers in advance (she and Father were having one of their regular disputes over how much freedom the boy should have), so I was able to cut Father out of the deal altogether.

The Vette was so powerful and jittery, like a feisty thoroughbred knocking against the starting gate, I had trouble holding it on the road when I floored the accelerator and laid rubber on Route 66 back into Yukon. But this was exactly the feeling I wanted. Within half an hour, the cherry sports car had fulfilled my most urgent adolescent dream: Lila Ruzicka was strapped into the bucket seat beside me. On our way to El Reno—a trip that usually took about fifteen minutes, but which we made in eight—Lila leaned over the console, her legendary breasts pressing against my quaking shoulder, and planted her lips on mine. A one hundred mile per hour kiss.

The road ahead was a dazzling blur.

Later that afternoon when I pulled the Stingray into the garage and shut down the rumbling V-8, Father was waiting for me. I could tell from the stunned look in his eyes he was more than disappointed. He was humiliated. When I stepped out of the Stingray his eyes met me with such a look of rage and abhorrence that I almost shrank back against the fiberglass fender, afraid he might say *No, you can't have this.*

In all our conflicts I'd never lifted a finger against Father, but I would fight for this car. I'd paid for it with my own money. I wanted it. I wanted to be judged by it. If the old man tried to take it from me, I'd . . .

But all he did was stare incredulously at the cherry fiberglass skin of the Stingray and say, "So this is what you spent your money on."

I gathered myself up to my full height—I was a good four inches taller than he, even then—and replied, "What'd you expect?"

He swung his gaze from the car to me and said, "I expect only one thing from you."

I waited for the rest, but instead of finishing his statement he turned his back on me and walked into the house. "You only expect *what?*" I yelled after him.

Mother loved the Corvette. "It's gorgeous," she said, snuggling down in the passenger bucket that same afternoon. I took her for a ride—slower, seat belts buckled— north toward Piedmont, and she defiled the virgin ash tray with the butt of a Winston. "I'll swan, what am I doing?" she exclaimed when the unlit cigarette suddenly appeared between her middle and index fingers. "I shouldn't smoke up your pretty new car."

"Go right ahead," I said. It was the first time I'd ever seen her light a cigarette out of nervousness. I didn't care about that, or the fact that the smoke would ruin the clean vinyl smell of the Stingray's jet black interior. She had something she wanted to say, and if a cigarette would help her get the words out, that was OK by me. Out of the corner of my right eye I watched her roll down the passenger window, then turn her head and let the turbulent air just beyond her shoulder suck the first puff right off her lips.

"You know," she said at last, turning back to face me, "you and your Father have turned out to be very different sorts of people."

"No kidding."

Mother's eyes returned to the road before us. It was a warm afternoon for October, and she was wearing shorts. She took her palms and pushed them over the tops of her bare thighs as if she were smoothing a skirt. "I think he can accept that," she said. "He's going to have to."

"You're right about that."

"But you know, you could make it a whole lot easier for him."

I bit my lower lip. "How's that?"

Mother inhaled, blew another stream out the window, then stabbed the less than half-smoked cigarette out in the ashtray. "This car . . ."

"I'm not giving up this car," I interrupted her. "No matter what."

Mother shifted her voice down an octave. "You don't have to tell me that. I recognize a Kellerman when I see one."

I felt my face and neck begin to blush.

"I'm just saying you can make it easier for him to accept it," she went on. "The car, I mean. And the fact that you're different."

I heaved a sigh. "But you just said . . ." I let the words trail off.

Mother let her eyes follow the passing blur of an oil tank truck. "Did Frank ever tell you about his first car?"

"The Moon?"

"The Moon was his second car."

I frowned. "Which one was first?"

"Not any of them he has now. His very first car was a wreck he restored in an old barn at the bottom of Fairmont

Street in Kansas City. Actually, 'restored' is the wrong word. He *rebuilt* the entire car from scraps."

This didn't surprise me. "So what kind of car was it?"

"I don't know, some kind of Ford. I never saw it with my own eyes, you understand. This was before I knew your father. But he told me all about how he built that car with his own two hands, piece by piece. It was the first thing he ever did in his life that he was proud of. It took one whole year. When he'd finished it, the first thing he did was show it to your Grandpa Kellerman. And you know what your grandpa did?"

An old fearful curiosity reasserted itself in the back of my brain. But I merely shrugged.

"He chopped the car to pieces with an ax."

"What?" I glanced over at her to make sure I'd heard correctly. "*Why?* Why'd he do that?"

Mother's voice was flat and calm. "Because he hadn't given your father permission to build it, that's why."

I paused to take this in. Grandpa Kellerman had been dead six years now, and I still knew almost nothing about him. I suddenly recalled the one word description Father had given of him when I'd asked what Grandpa Kellerman was like: *Mean.*

"That's crazy," I said. "And meaner than mean ... What did Dad do when grandpa chopped up the car?"

Mother shook her head. "Nothing. He just watched."

I tried to picture this scene in my mind's eye, but couldn't. It was too horrible.

"Your father hated him after that. I believe that's why he wouldn't let us go to your grandpa's funeral."

I tried to imagine what Father had felt all these years. But I couldn't. Maybe I wasn't capable of a hatred that deep and profound. I cleared my throat and said, "He talks about his cars so much, how come he never told me about his first one?"

Mother shrugged. "I don't know. Too painful, maybe."

"He told you."

For a few moments neither of us said anything further as Mother thought about this. Finally, she leaned toward me and said, "I can't answer that. But I do know one thing. Whatever else you may think about your father, I want you to consider this: He hasn't said you can't keep the Corvette."

I eased off the gas. The road ahead was blurry again, but in a different way than it had been with Lila. "So what should I do to make things easier for him?"

"Just don't confront him with it. This car, I mean. Best thing to do is just let him ignore it for now. Maybe he'll get used to it."

I thought it over and decided to take her advice. After all, if Father could adjust to living with bees, he could damn well get used to my Corvette. And if he had to ignore the car to get used to it, well, that was fine with me. I'd just ignore him ignoring my car. Ignoring things was a craft we'd both mastered long ago.

* * *

Six months went by. Father and I did not speak of the Corvette. In fact, we hardly spoke at all. Whenever I pulled the Stingray into the garage I always raced the engine before shutting it off. I let the four hundred twenty-seven cubic inches of V-8 scream what I dared not say to the old man. I'd decided that silence was the one thing he expected of me.

His own silence was more powerful than mine. Now I understood why. He'd practiced the power of silence for many years more than I, on his own father. He'd perfected it. When he finally decided to use this power on me, I felt its effects instantly. He took no notice of the Corvette; in his universe it didn't exist. The invisible barrier between us grew thicker, more impenetrable, day by day. I believe that as time passed we were actually becoming invisible to each other. That's the ultimate effect of successfully ignoring something: It begins to disappear. But I still *felt* his presence as we circled each other blindly like two submarines gliding noiselessly through deep water. I think we both knew a collision was inevitable.

It happened one Saturday morning in late April of the new year. I was changing a record on the stereo in my bedroom, removing the Association (I was about ready to remove them altogether from my list of tolerable bands) and replacing them with a Bob Dylan, when Father loomed in the doorway. I knew instantly what was happening. Father was wearing his blue overalls and a frustrated but determined expression, his brow clenched like a fist. A magnetic storm was disrupting the galaxy, a window through space and time had opened, and we were both suddenly visible.

"I need some help," he said.

Careful, I warned myself. I turned away from the stereo and faced him. "With what?"

He stepped into the center of the bedroom, onto the fake Persian throw rug that lay directly beneath my ceiling poster of the Rolling Stones. "I need you to help me load that two-ton air conditioner on the Jimmie Truck."

The words instantly brought back the lore of Father's workshop: Two-ton meant two thousand BTUs. British thermal units. For a moment I was back inside his universe, projected at warp speed through an invisible portal in the vacuum of space. Then I remembered my own place.

"Where is it?"

Father's jaw set itself like a gear locking into place. Then it moved. "In the schoolhouse."

I'd been preparing for this, for the moment when one of us would force the issue and either make the break between us permanent—or swing the invisible door wide open once again, maybe for the last time. I had set speeches I'd practiced in my head. I was ready, I thought, to take a step toward Father, through the portal.

But now that the moment had come, it was charged with negative energy. I forgot my set speeches, and wavered.

"It's too heavy for me to lift by myself," Father said when I hesitated. "Your mother's in town shopping, and it's too heavy for her to help me with anyway. And you know it."

It was his tone more than my long-standing fear of his bees that made me dig my heels into the fake Persian rug beneath our feet. He'd hurled the words at me like a handful of mud.

"So get somebody else to help you," I heard myself reply. "Go get Cletus's daddy; he helped you carry it in."

"Why should I call a neighbor when my own son is standing three feet away from me? It'll take two minutes of your goddamn precious time." As he spat these words in my direction, he dipped his head to glare at me above the thick glass of his bifocals resting on his fat misshapened nose. His beady gray eyes glistened with resentment. Or was it fear?

I took a breath and softened my voice. I wanted to take that step. "Dad, you know how I feel about those bees—"

"*Damn* it!" he snapped, cutting me off. "I've told you a thousand times: If you leave 'em alone they won't sting you."

I stared at the sweat beading his bald head and said nothing. The door was closing, but I had to be calm—both of us had to be calm—for me to step through.

"It's got nothing to do with the damn bees," he blurted before I had steadied myself enough to reply. "It's ME you don't want to deal with."

Calm. Stay calm, I chanted silently. But I could bear neither Father's words nor the look on his face. I rolled my eyes up toward Mick Jagger and turned back toward the stereo.

"Don't turn your back on me! By God, I've never forced you to do anything, but you're coming over to that schoolhouse right now and help me load that air conditioner in the pickup!"

Suddenly everything shifted into fast-forward. I felt his hand grab my left arm and yank me around. Instead of resisting, I spun toward him, my right fist clenched. He did not anticipate the punch. My knuckles struck the point of his chin, a perfect right hook—and he went down.

Until this moment I had never touched Father in anger.

He landed heavily on his butt in the corner next to the chest of drawers. An instant later, his bifocals, jarred free by the blow, smacked the bare wood floor of the hallway just outside my bedroom doorway.

For a moment I thought he was out cold, though his eyes were open, bulging and white. Then he stirred, looked directly at me, and blinked. After a moment or two his gaze shifted away from my face and drifted around the room, as if he were trying to piece together where he was, and how he got here. When his eyes finally fixed on me again, his vision seemed to turn back into his own head.

He knew.

Bracing his back against the wall, Father rose. I stood where I was, frozen in place like I was the one backed into the corner. By the time Father reached his feet, everything was different.

"I'm sorry," I said. "I didn't mean to do that." The words lay flat and pathetic on my tongue.

He didn't respond. He turned his back and walked out of the bedroom.

I jerked out of my paralysis and came to the doorway. "You still want me to help you move that air conditioner?"

The shake of his head was barely visible. He didn't break stride as he bent over to retrieve his glasses from the floor. While his silhouette receded down the dim hallway toward the kitchen, I felt the long silence between us deepen. A moment later the screen door banged shut.

* * *

Half an hour later I climbed into the cherry Stingray and drove down to the clinic in Yukon, taking special care with the four-speed shift.

"Well now," Dr. Enos proclaimed as he examined the red, rapidly swelling area behind my largest protruding knuckle. "We'll X-ray it, but I can tell you right now it's not a sprain. Looks like you've fractured the bone that connects your middle finger to your wrist. Busted it good, I'd say."

I nodded. The pain was like a white hot branding rod driven deep into my hand. But I was having trouble feeling it.

"How'd you do this?"

When I didn't answer, he looked up and studied my face. Dr. Enos had been my doctor since the day after I was born. I'd never clammed up on him before.

"Curly . . . What happened to you?"

I considered the question carefully, as carefully as I'd ever considered anything. Finally, I looked Dr. Enos in the eye and said, "I missed the old man's nose."

* * *

It took another hour and a half to X-ray, reset the bone, and construct the plaster cast.

"You need somebody to drive you?" Dr. Enos asked.

"Nope. I can manage."

I shifted the four speed with my left hand while pinning the wheel against my right shoulder to hold the Corvette on course. I drove slowly, watching the road like I'd never watched it before, keeping my mind on the task at hand. The pain, throbbing beneath the cast despite the pills Dr. Enos had given me, helped me focus. This time when I pulled into the garage, I didn't feel like racing the engine. I turned it off and sat in the black leather bucket, listening to the big 427 V-8 *tick, tick* as the metal cooled and contracted—something else I remembered from my apprenticeship. Mother was in the kitchen putting groceries away. Through the wall I could hear tin cans clunk into place in the cabinet. She must have heard the Corvette, but didn't come out. Which meant she didn't yet know what had happened.

Father had to be in the schoolhouse.

I sat in the Stingray and rested the cast on the side of the passenger bucket. Now that the deed was done, the invisible door closed, I could turn my thoughts to the future. In another month I'd graduate. In the fall I'd be heading off to Oklahoma State University in Stillwater with Eddie Hacker and Lila and Cletus, who had a football scholarship. The new universe, the one I hadn't really charted yet, lay in that direction. The old universes were already drifting away somewhere behind me. Everything seemed set.

I decided I might as well go in and let Mother see the cast, get that over with. Climbing out of the Corvette I glanced back through the wide double car doorway of the garage, and a movement caught my eye: a small figure crouching behind the rear fender of the Studebaker Silver Hawk, nearest in line beneath the tin roof of Father's carport.

Mrs. Zucha.

And I realized things weren't quite set after all. I had one thing left to do.

As I approached the carport it looked like Mrs. Zucha

was gazing at the schoolhouse, lost in some distant memory of her wedding day—or perhaps transfixed by a phantom vision of her dead Hubert walking around in my father's graying body somewhere behind the dusky window glass. I felt a sudden pang of jealousy when I realized it was Father and not me who compelled Mrs. Zucha to return, again and again for the last six years following her fall, to this place. She must have been mesmerized by the bees, for she didn't spot me watching her gray head slowly turn in my direction, her eyes a shiny black as they followed the flight of Father's honeys from crack to field. Her gaze was about to swing back toward the limestone wall to follow a returning honey hunter, when she discovered me standing no more than half a dozen steps away.

She froze, her black eyes locked onto my own. Beneath her gray dress, the same gray dress she had worn on the cliff so many years ago, her bony shoulders trembled.

Calm, I thought. I hadn't been this close to Mrs. Zucha since Mother and Father and I visited her as she slept, unaware of our presence, in her private room at Baptist Memorial. I searched her face for some sign that she recognized me. But her eyes expressed only fear. I wanted to communicate with her in our old way, without words. For a moment I considered lifting my arms to catch the rising breeze beneath my invisible wing feathers. But this was not about flying. I would have to speak.

In my softest voice I asked: "Do you want to go inside?"

The black eyes regarded me without change.

Slowly, I raised my left arm and pointed beyond the row of automobiles to the schoolhouse. "There. Do you want to go inside?"

She did not turn her head to follow my gesture, but her eyes grew like black holes in space. Was there really anything inside the old schoolhouse for her? A memory? A ghost she could see only through the body of my father? It wasn't for me to say.

"The bees," I said. "They won't hurt you."

At the mention of "bees," she ducked her head an inch and looked quickly up and around, as if one of them might have been about to divebomb her.

I shook my head. "It's OK. My father's inside the school-house. They're his bees. His honeys. He won't let them hurt you."

Now the black eyes contracted into a squint. She was listening.

"If I ask him, he'll let you come inside the schoolhouse. You can go right on in and look around."

Did I see something else in Mrs. Zucha's eyes now? Was I getting through?

"If you like, I'll walk you over to the door and call Father." No, I thought. These were not the right words. This time I knew the right words, but could I bring myself to say them?

"I mean, call . . . Hubert."

Her eyes brightened, gleamed like distant planets.

"Do you want to come with me?"

Her head tilted to the side like a nervous crow angling to keep a watchful eye on a potential predator—or an elderly woman who was listening with great care. *It's all right*, I tried to say with my eyes.

"Here," I said aloud, and, as casually as I could manage, extended my hand. "I'll walk you over—"

As I said these words an errant bee, its internal compass demagnetized by the recent disturbance in the cosmos, flew between us. I glanced at the bee for an instant and Mrs. Zucha broke free.

"Wait!" I cried after her. But she was already gone, racing like a girl toward the road, then across it, into Orville's northern pasture. She was out of sight quickly, down the slope of the pasture into the wooded area by the creek. But not, it seemed, toward the willow tree nor our old take-off point above the cliff. Her path took her further south, toward some secret place that was hers alone.

When she had disappeared from sight, I turned and scanned the row of Father's automobiles, a lineup I now realized was incomplete. Headlights and grills leered at passing motorists like the faces of gargoyles. My gaze lingered for a few moments on the bright purple fenders of the Moon Prince of Windsor at the far end of the line, then moved on, finally settling on the more distant gray limestone walls that concealed Father's workshop.

I had no reason, no purpose in mind. I approached the schoolhouse and picked up the humming pulse of Father's honeys hard at work. I knew only that he was holed up inside there, doing whatever he did in his private sanctuary, protected by his personal guardians. I walked around to the west side and found the door wide open. I stopped. Bees, hundreds of them, flew in and out of the doorway in precise lines not more than three feet in front of my face. Hundreds more bees crawled on boxes and tools and general debris lying just inside the door.

I stood a good ten feet from the entrance and shivered. "Dad!"

No answer. The hum was much louder here; it echoed from within. I considered the possibility that he couldn't hear me through the wall of sound that stood between us. From the spot where I stood trembling I couldn't see him either, just towers of boxes, mounds of auto parts, stacks of future projects: lawn mower engines, broken toilets, electric can openers, an old Maytag washing machine standing on four short skinny legs. From a different angle, he might have been in plain view. Or perhaps it was just me who couldn't see him. Perhaps in our separate universes we had finally become invisible to each other, as well as mute.

"DAD!"

Nothing. The massive hum continued without interruption: Work went on, bees flew in and out. Oh, he was in there, all right. My father, the man who was not Hubert. From somewhere inside I heard the bang and scrape of metal against metal. I waited maybe a minute, but Father didn't answer.

The truth was he didn't need to. There was nothing to be said anyway. Any mechanic worth his salt understood that for the important jobs there were no manuals to read, no words to explain what had to be done. One learned by doing. I didn't know if I would be stepping back into the past or into an altered future. It didn't matter. My road ran through that door.

About the Author

Steve Heller grew up near Yukon, Oklahoma, where the events of this story take place. His first book, *The Man Who Drank a Thousand Beers*, has been called "A Hawaiian *Winesburg, Ohio.*" *The Automotive History of Lucky Kellerman*, Heller's first novel, was a selection of Book-of-the-Month Club and Quality Paperback Book Club, and received the Friends of American Writers First Prize Award. Heller's short stories and essays have appeared in many journals and national anthologies. His writings have earned various honors, including an NEA Individual Artist Fellowship Grant in Fiction, two O. Henry Awards, the Kansas Artists Fellowship in Fiction, and the Kansas Governor's Arts Award. Heller teaches creative writing at Kansas State University in Manhattan, where he lives with his wife, nonfiction writer Sheyene Foster Heller.